ADRIAN

L for L

Best wishes

Adrian

ANOTHER SMALL PRESS
No. 2

ISBN 978-0-9957127-1-3

Published in Great Britain by Another Small Press, 2023

www.anothersmallpress.net
Cover design by Fine Fine Lines

Adrian Bean was born in Cardiff in 1960 and grew up in Nottinghamshire. He has worked as a director and writer in theatre, television and radio for over forty years, and is fascinated by aeroplanes. In 1995 he directed the BBC's acclaimed and ground-breaking radio drama *Bomber*, adapted from the novel by Len Deighton, and broadcast in real time on Radio 4. He is a member of Fosseway Writers based in Newark, and is currently writing a book about the death of his uncle in a mid-air collision over Nottinghamshire in 1941. *What Happened* will be published by Another Small Press.

Contents

Preface

In the summer of 2022, I found myself unexpectedly researching an incident that took place in rural Nottinghamshire during the Second World War. My curiosity had been aroused following a chance conversation with my mother, who told me that an uncle of mine had been killed at an RAF bomber station only a few miles from the village where I grew up, and where she still lived. Not really knowing anything about this uncle, but intrigued nevertheless, I started to dig, and quite literally, eventually unearthed evidence of a story which involved, in all, the deaths of eight brave men.

As is often the case with stories, those which one writes as well as those which are uncovered, there were unexpected twists along the way. My Uncle Bill, it turned out, did not die at RAF Syerston, as my mother had told me, but over a small village some seven miles away, in a mid-air collision between the Airspeed Oxford trainer he and a fellow u/t[1] pilot were flying, and a Wellington bomber, flown by an all-Polish crew stationed at Syerston.

The story of that tragic accident, and of how I unearthed the details of it, is the subject of another book.[2] However, in the course of my research, I wanted to find out if any people who lived in or near the area where it happened had information or memories about the incident (admittedly a

---

[1] Pilot Under Training

[2] *What Happened*, by Adrian Bean. Another Small Press 2024

faint hope, as it happened over 80 years ago). This included doing a letter drop, which involved me pushing leaflets through letter boxes, outlining the story I was researching along with my contact details. The letter drop provided some fascinating and invaluable leads which I was able to follow up and which are discussed in the other book; it also led to another meeting, which in the end didn't have any direct relevance to the story of my Uncle Bill and is therefore not included in that book, but without which this book would not exist.

Several days after the letter drop, I received a letter from a woman explaining that she hoped she might be of assistance in my research into Syerston as she had been a WAAF there during the war. The letter invited me to meet her at her home, in a village a couple of miles away from where the accident had occurred; she gave a specific date and time, and although this clashed with a previous engagement, it sounded too good an opportunity to miss, and so a few days later, we met.

For reasons which I hope will become clear to the reader of these stories, I have chosen not to reveal the woman's identity. However, it seems rude to only refer to her by her pronouns, so I will give her a name for the purposes of this introduction and call her Ivy. We spent a very pleasant afternoon together, in the small cottage where she lived alone, drinking tea from the pot and eating sandwiches which Ivy had made using tomatoes and lettuce grown in her own garden. She was, at the time of our meeting, as the reader can imagine, in her late nineties, but fit and living a relatively independent life, in full possession of all her mental faculties; the product, in part no doubt, of her wartime experience.

Ivy had been posted to RAF Syerston in late 1942, when the Lancasters of 106 Squadron were stationed there, commanded by Guy Gibson, who would later go on to lead 617 Squadron in the daring Dam Busters raid. She was less than glowing in her reminiscences of Gibson, who she described as 'a difficult man, very complicated, and not as popular as his legend would suggest', but full of praise for the Station Commander Gus Walker, who went by the nickname of 'the one-armed bandit.' As part of my research, I had read the story of how Walker came to lose his arm, but Ivy was actually there when it happened, and told me in detail about how he had rushed from the Watch Office when he saw a waiting Lancaster on fire, and tried to clear the bomber of its load of incendiaries before the 4000lb Cookie it was carrying exploded. The Cookie did in fact go off, and the Station Commander was hurled across the airfield, lucky to lose only an arm. (Apparently, according to Ivy, the possibly apocryphal story about Walker complaining that he never found the missing arm bearing the glove from his favourite pair was true). Ivy also remembered meeting the renowned broadcaster David Dimbleby, who flew from Syerston with Gibson on the first Lancaster raid on Berlin, recording his experiences for a landmark BBC radio broadcast, and was most impressed, saying the man obviously had 'guts', although most of the contents of his guts ended up around the Lancaster's fuselage when Gibson insisted on going around the heavily defended target for a third time to find the aiming point.

These stories, as well as her many other more personal and less dramatic memories, were fascinating, but sadly largely irrelevant to my research, because I was only interested in the year 1941, when the airfield was home to the Polish aircrews of 304 and 305 Squadrons. I explained that it was a crew from No 305 'Ziemia Wielkopolska' (Land of Greater Poland) Bomber Squadron that had died in the mid-air collision with my Uncle Bill's aircraft, and therefore I was only concerned with the period before Ivy's time at Syerston.

She asked me more about my Uncle Bill, and what I had already discovered about how he and the other seven men died that day in June 1941, and I told her as much as I knew; that the Wellington bomber had taken off for a training flight hours before it was due to take part in a large effort on the marshalling yards at Osnabruck in Germany, and that it had collided in poor visibility with the Oxford trainer that my

Uncle Bill and his friend were flying, 900 feet above the village just down the road. I told her that there had been no enquiry into the accident, that I hoped to be able to organise some kind of reunion involving family members, maybe even erect a memorial, and that I was going to write a book about it.

Looking back, I would like to say that at that moment I registered a faint reaction on Ivy's face, as if my story had reminded her of something, but if I did, I would be lying. Ivy continued to pour tea and to chat about her life after the war; about how there had been 'someone' but things hadn't worked out and she never married; how she had settled in this village and got a job as a teacher; that there were some distant relatives somewhere in Canada but that they had long since lost contact and that she was, effectively, the last of her family line. Without any drama she told me that when she died, as she expected to in the not-too-distant future, her memories would go with her, and she was glad to have had the opportunity of sharing some of them with me.

When it was time for me to leave, she wished me luck with my research and hoped my mother would do well, but just as I was getting into my car, she stopped me and hurried back into the cottage. A few minutes later she re-emerged, carrying a plain brown cardboard box, tied with string, which she handed to me, saying she wanted me to have it. I asked her what was in the box, and she shrugged, saying it was some 'odds and sods from her time at Syerston', and repeated that she wanted me to have them, and hoped I might find a use for them. I explained again that sadly her experiences all post-dated the time I was writing about, but she insisted I keep the box anyway, and giving me no chance to argue, hurried away saying it looked like rain and she had washing to bring in.

I am ashamed to say that the box remained unopened for several months, sitting amongst a gathering pile of books, maps and papers which represented my current obsession – pinpointing the exact locations where the two aircraft had come down. My days were filled with excursions accompanying Tony, my tame metal detectorist friend, as we

10

searched the fields where, according to various sources, physical evidence of the Wellington and Oxford would be found. Then one day, when our planned expedition had been called off due to bad weather, I was at something of a loose end, and my eye fell on the box.

I made a cup of coffee, sat down, and untied the string. Inside, it was much as Ivy had suggested – a collection of papers, including documents relating to her career in the WAAF, telegrams, an identity card and ration book. There were photographs, of a plain young girl in WAAF uniform who I recognised as an eighteen-year-old Ivy; others including gangs of jolly WAAFs, on and off-duty, some with smiling uniformed men, arms around waists, always smoking, even a few with Lancasters or bomb trolleys in the background. There were bundles of letters and postcards, tied with ribbon, faded newspaper cuttings, train tickets, theatre programmes and other items that must have had special memories or significance for Ivy, but which, as I expected, would be of little use to me and my book. Towards the bottom of the box, I found a number of photographs of a young airman as well, wearing a nervous smile and pilot's wings on his chest. Finally, at the very bottom, was a single large plain manilla envelope.

The envelope contained seventy-odd foolscap pages of close typescript, the short stories contained in this book. There was nothing to say who the author was – 'No names, no pack drill', as Ivy would have said in her clipped, rather old-fashioned accent – just the titles. I started to read them, terrified in case I should damage the fragile pages, and was immediately transported to 1943, and a windswept bomber airfield in Nottinghamshire.

Although they are set on a bomber station during the dark days of the war, they are not really war stories in the strictest sense. There is very little in the way of exciting combat, or heroic 'derring-do' in the skies over Germany. These stories are about the day-to-day life of a bomber station, and are, for the most part, simple tales about ordinary men and women, told with understatement, a dark humour and repressed emotion, all things which I remembered about Ivy from our one meeting. Which makes me think, *were they written by her?* They could have been, as she certainly had an extensive knowledge of life (and death) on a bomber station. Or maybe they were written by the pilot in the photographs, who I assumed was a boyfriend, possibly the one with whom 'things hadn't worked out'. Perhaps Hobson, the cheerful WAAF who appears in two of the stories, was Ivy in disguise? The station, although not identified as Syerston, certainly could have been based on it, and the nearby town is most probably Newark, given the detailed descriptions of both in the first story in the collection, *The Committee of Adjustment*.[3]

I will never know the answers to these questions, because when I drove round to Ivy's cottage to ask her about the stories, I was too late. Ivy had died, found collapsed in her garden by a neighbour, only a fortnight earlier.

So what should I do with the stories, and the other items in the box? The obvious answer was to donate the whole collection to a museum or archive, where they could be kept safe for posterity, and appreciated by historians and the public. The letters were extremely personal, and very revealing of Ivy and her lovers, and I worried at first about how she would have reacted to the idea of them being 'on display', but on reflection I decided that they were too valuable a resource to remain hidden any longer, and offered them to the Newark Air Museum, where they now reside.

But what of the stories? Letters are private, and not usually intended for publication, but stories are different. For a start they were (I assume) fictional, and although based on a lived reality, they were probably intended for a public audience; in a sense, therefore, they would cease to exist if they were not read, and not just by me. I wrote to several London publishers, each of whom I thought would be interested in

---

[3] The station could also be RAF Swinderby. Like Syerston it was built as part of the RAF's pre-war expansion, but its location north of Newark makes it a less convincing candidate.

taking the stories, but they were unanimously rejected; not, I think, because of their quality, but because of 'the market'. I was told that it was difficult to see how just four stories would be economically viable for publication – if there were more, say eight or nine, it might be different, or if they were published alongside the letters and photographs, and a biography of Ivy, they might be more marketable. But I have already said how I thought Ivy would have felt about that, and reminding myself that she had insisted they were mine to do as I pleased with, I decided to look elsewhere.

Which is where Another Small Press comes in. This small publisher specialises in supporting local writers, and the man at the helm, Martin Costello, jumped at the chance of giving these stories the exposure we both thought they deserved. He had one reservation: why had Ivy not sought to publish them in the years following the war, when there was a plethora of stories about the RAF on the bookshelves? Paul Brickhill's *The Dam Busters*, or his story of Douglas Bader in *Reach For The Sky*, or the novels of Neville Shute and HE Bates were good examples of the genre, and testified to the public demand for stories about the RAF. Perhaps she thought these were too personal to publish, given their probable provenance, and wanted to forget the war and the pain of those years. Or, and this seemed to me to be a fair comment, maybe she felt that some of the sentiments and ideas expressed in the stories about Bomber Command's wartime role were too negative and would be unpopular with the generation of post-war readers. It is well known that public revulsion and guilt at the mass destruction wrought by Bomber Harris's campaign meant that after the war the men of Bomber Command were overlooked when it came to handing out medals and accolades. Ivy may have felt that whatever the truth or otherwise of the arguments voiced by some of the characters in the stories, she or her colleagues would feel uncomfortable being associated with these views. I saw Martin's point, but we both agreed that if published now, the stories would be received by an audience with a very different perspective on the Second World War, and Bomber Command's controversial role in it.

I have edited them, but only by simplifying the rather over-elaborate punctuation that tended to characterise prose style in the 1940s; some capitals, commas and semicolons have been removed, and double speech marks replaced with singles, and I hope the reader (and the author) will forgive me for taking this liberty. More controversially perhaps, I have also included an extra story, from which the collection takes its name; *L for Lanc*, which is my personal contribution to the collection. I apologise in advance if the reader feels that in matters of style and subject it sits uncomfortably with stories that are of the 1940s. It goes without saying that it doesn't bear comparison with the other stories, whoever wrote them, but I hope that the reader will please read it with this in mind – that is written by someone who never experienced war, like my WAAF and her friends, but who continues to be fascinated by it, and should be read in that context.

Adrian Bean. Newark. May 2023

The Committee of Adjustment

'Same again?'

He was aware of her voice but did not look up, his eyes fixed on the small pile of letters sitting on the bar table.

'Same again, duck?'

He looked up. 'Oh, sorry, I – yes, please. Thank you.'

The barmaid leant back on her heels and fixed him with a stare. 'You alright duck?'

He considered. 'Yes. Thank you.'

She held his look for a second, nodded, then turned and walked away. His eyes followed her to the bar, and he noticed a group of young airmen, apparently refusing to let her pass until she gave them The Password. Despite maintaining a pretence of mild annoyance, she clearly enjoyed the attention of the airmen, each of whom was young enough to be her son.

He looked again at the letters and checked his watch. Gone ten o'clock. He lit a cigarette, noticing that there was only one left in the packet, and inhaled deeply, triggering a spasm of coughing. Reaching into his inside pocket he pulled out a leather case containing a green Bakelite fountain pen and a small dagger-like letter opener. With the practised skill of a surgeon, he inserted it into the envelope. The thin wartime economy standard paper slit open neatly and he pulled out three folded pages, ignoring the slight shaking of the paper, the effect of a tremble which had appeared following his recent visit to the station Medical Officer. He checked the envelope to ensure that it contained nothing else, turning the folded pages over, but nothing fell out.

He began reading:

Somewhere in England!
September 29th, 1943

Dearest Mum and Dad,

Please excuse my handwriting as I'm working by the dim light of a blacked-out train carriage, stuck somewhere between Darlington and York - at least that's what the Guard says – he's what Dad would call 'a very officious type' who likes to keep that kind of information to himself just to impress. Needless to say, he didn't impress me – I gave him a flash of the new air gunner brevet on my tunic, and he soon shut up!

Apparently, there is an air raid alert and so the train has been standing in a tunnel for over an hour now, with no indication of when we might be on the move again, so I thought it would be a good use of my time if I started to write you a letter.

In my last, I told you about the Operational Training Unit I was stationed at up in Scotland, and about the Wimpys we were getting our final training on. Well, the Wimpy is a splendid two-engine bomber, marvellously rugged, and bristling with guns, but according to our instructors (rather terrifying chaps, most of whom have done their tour of thirty ops[4] over Germany) the Wellington is most definitely Yesterday's Thing. All they talk about is the Lancaster, a super new aircraft with four engines and a bomb-bay the size of a cricket pitch! Think of how many bombs we can drop on German factories from one of those. (Don't worry Dad – I'm not revealing any military secrets. The Germans know exactly what a punch the Lancaster packs, as they've been on the receiving end of it for months now).

The whisky glass hit the table with a sharp clunk.

'One double. Sorry about the wait, duck. I got distracted.' Her expression changed, the thin, painted-on eyebrows moving closer together. 'If you don't mind me

---

[4] Operations: successfully completed flights or sorties against the primary or secondary target.

saying, you look like you could do with it.'

He reached for his wallet, but she stopped him. 'Don't worry duck, I'll put it on the slate. You'll still be here at the end of the week I dare say, unlike some.'

He followed her glance to the group of young airmen, now engaged in turning the pages of a copy of the local paper into paper aeroplanes and taking bets on who could fly his the furthest across the bar. There was a roar as one of them managed to land an aeroplane in the fire, and it was quickly consumed in a burst of flames.

'Boys, eh?' The barmaid laughed, and he noticed that her cheeks were slightly flushed, and she seemed a little breathless. He felt suddenly very old. It was a long time since he had affected a woman like those young men did. He reached for his cigarettes.

'I'm almost out,' he said. 'Bring me some over, would you? Ten Piccadilly.'

She raised a single painted eyebrow: 'What did your last slave die of?' A sudden stab of emotion caught him in the chest. She meant no harm by it, he knew, it was just a quip, but suddenly he wanted to tell her how unfair it was of her to make jokes after everything that had happened to him today, and yesterday and all the other days; what he had heard, and seen, and done, how it was eating away at his soul and he really didn't know if he could carry on any longer.

But she had already turned away and was threading her way through the gaggle of young men again.

...Anyway, with these grizzled old Instructor types it's 'Lancs this' and 'Lancs that', so I can't tell you how excited I was when I got my orders telling me I was joining a Lancaster squadron for operational duties! Actually, it was when I was chatting to Anne (one of the WAAFs who packs our parachutes) that I learned I was to be flying on Lancasters. I'd mentioned to her the name of the station where I was being posted, and she said that her sister's fiancé was stationed nearby. Anyway, the point of the story is that my new squadron operates Lancasters, and so it looks like my wish

will come true!

Well, the train has started up, and it seems we are finally moving. I'll sign off now and post this to you as soon as I can (I'm all out of stamps).

When I get home I promise to take Mum for a long walk around Alexandra Park so she can show her brave son off to all the neighbours in his smart blue uniform (you know you want to, Mum!). Give Meg a hug from me (but not too many treats!) and tell her when I see her we'll go for her favourite walk along the canal.

With all best wishes,
Your loving son,
Harry xx

P.S. The old lady sitting opposite has just told me off for straining my eyes in the poor light! Little does she know I have perfect night vision.

He sat for a few moments as an image came into his head, of a boy in rolled-up shirtsleeves, a cow lick of hair flopping over his eyes, carefully folding the letter he'd just written and sliding it into the envelope. Except the boy wasn't called Harry, but Philip, and he was sitting in a tent under the blazing North African sun.

'One of your boys?' She was back, gesturing with the packet of Piccadillys towards the letter in his hand.

'One normally reads these things back in the office, on the station. Time's so short and one is always in a hurry, it seems...' As he put the letter back into its envelope, he was aware of her watching him. He felt he had to say something.

'I suppose, tonight, I just needed to...'

'It's alright, duck, you don't need to tell me.' She tapped the side of her nose. 'I heard what happened.'

He lit a cigarette, taking a deep, gratifying drag on it. What did she mean by that? He was about to ask her, but she was already gone.

Like the first, the second letter was addressed to a Mr and Mrs J Greenhalgh at an address in Oldham, and again, unstamped. He slit the envelope open, repeated the ritual of shaking it out, and began to read:

RAF Station S-------
Nottinghamshire
September 30th, 1943

Dearest Mum and Dad,

Well, I have finally arrived at my new home, after a journey that took over eighteen hours - I could have walked it in less time! Apparently, according to one chap in the carriage, we actually went past our destination twice, because of the diversions, before finally arriving from Leicester, of all places!

Having made our acquaintance on the subject of Night Vision, the dear old lady and I had some interesting conversations during the waits, mostly about her sons, one of whom is a high-up in some cushy War Ministry office in London and the other in a POW camp somewhere in Germany. What a situation for her. Apparently the one in the POW camp was also in the RAF, on Blenheims, and was posted Missing back in 1940, but she only found out that he was alive and being held prisoner six months later! She's had a couple of Red Cross postcards from him since, but they don't say much other than that he is well and uninjured. Poor soul.

Anyway, we said cheerio when I finally got off and I waved her goodbye. It was four o'clock by now and the Station Master told me I could get a bus 'down the Fosse' [5] *that would take me to the gates of the aerodrome, if I didn't mind the wait (ha ha!), so I thought I would have a cup of tea and a bite to eat but unfortunately the tearoom was shut.*

From the railway station you can see the old castle ruins

---

[5] Fosse Way, the Roman road linking Exeter to Lincoln, passing through Newark.

rising above the river, and as the bus wasn't due for half an hour, I thought I would make the most of it and have a quick dekko around the place. Looking up at the ruined towers and thick walls you could almost imagine Roundheads and Cavaliers having a go at each other with pikes and swords hundreds of years ago. Strange that we are still fighting wars after all this time - you'd have thought we'd have learned something by now. Anyway, before I knew it, the church clock was chiming the half-hour and I had to hurry back to the train station or I'd miss my bus, so I'm afraid I missed posting your letter. I hope you won't mind waiting an extra day, but I'll wait until I get to the station and send them both together.

I can't tell you too much about the station for obvious reasons, but I must confess to feeling quite a thrill of excitement as I walked through the main gates. I actually think I might have grown an extra inch, feeling like quite the man marching in there, amongst all those other aircrew, knowing that at last I was now One Of Them. I hope you'd have been proud of me, both.

But I soon felt like the new boy at school again: it was all 'Report here', 'Go there', 'Find this' and 'Take that!' Before long, my head was in a whirl as I went from office to hut and back again, collecting a chit from here, drawing an item of kit from there. There is so much bumpf involved in joining a squadron, honestly you wouldn't believe. I tell you, if we bundled up just half a day's paperwork and dropped it on the Germans they'd be suing for peace in no time.

I'm lying on my bed, writing this, in a room with about twenty other beds, each with a metal locker and wooden bedside cabinet, all very neat and tidy, and I am lucky enough to be near a window. Every few minutes I hear the roar of engines approaching and look round to catch sight of a Lancaster overhead; I can't tell you how exciting it is to know that I will soon be up in one of those wonderful machines.

As luck would have it, as I finished that last sentence there was an almighty racket in the corridor outside and a couple of fellows stuck their heads in to ask if I was the new air gunner and that I should stooge over to the crew room where 'the Skipper' was waiting for me! They didn't hang around for me to follow, so I hope I can find it; I'll end this now and then I'm off to meet my new crew!

Your ever-loving son, (in a rush, as always!)
Harry xx

He uncapped his fountain pen and scored straight thick lines through several sentences and paragraphs, obscuring a few names, places, and minor technical references. He took a last drag on his cigarette and was suddenly overwhelmed by a fit of coughing. He'd been to the MO about a fortnight ago, with a nasty cough that just didn't seem to want to go away. After examining him, the MO offered him a cigarette, lit one himself, and said that he was recommending a chest X-Ray.

'Could be nothing. It'll probably all clear up in a matter of days but better safe than sorry.'

He'd put it out of his mind until the call from the MO's Orderly had come yesterday morning, asking him to report to the Station Sick Quarters. He'd gone over straight away, and didn't remember much about the actual conversation, other than the words lung and cancer.

'No doubt, I'm afraid,' said the MO. 'And it's fairly advanced. I could put you in for surgery, but there are risks associated with that for a chap of your age, and the results aren't always what one would hope for.'

When he finally spoke, his voice sounded weak, strangled.

'How long..?'

'Christmas,' said the MO. 'Possibly. You could still be here next spring with a bit of luck, it's hard to make an accurate prediction about these things. Sorry old chap.'

He nodded, his brain numb.

'I dare say you could do with a period of adjustment, get things in order. I'll sign you off now if you want, you've done more than enough for the squadron. You should spend some time at home, let Margaret make a fuss of you.'

He avoided the MO's look. Although they had known each other for years, he realised he hadn't actually ever got round to telling him that Margaret had left last Whitsun Holiday, and that since then she'd been living with her sister in Wrexham. He'd thought it better not to tell anyone at first, knowing how fast things get round the station.

The house had felt so empty for the first few weeks, and he nursed the faint hope each evening that he might come home to find her sitting in her armchair by the fire. But she hadn't come back. When the food cupboards ran empty, he took to eating his meals in the Officer's Mess at the station and started spending his evenings in the Saracen's Head in the town. There was often a fire in one of the smaller bars, and the regular barmaid was rather friendly, always ready with a story to make him laugh. It wasn't long before she had made up a slate for him; not that he needed it, but one evening he had found his wallet empty, and although initially embarrassed, soon the fact that he had a slate gave him a new-found sense of permanence. It meant they knew him there. That he belonged. That he would return.

Margaret leaving, he could take. He knew, after all, that he was at least half responsible for the breakdown of the marriage; more, if he was honest. It was the fact that his son had stopped talking to him that was hard to bear. He had become used to Philip's weekly letters from Tunisia, where he was a flight commander on Hurricanes. They had never been especially close, emotionally, when Philip was a kid, but war and the distance between them had, if anything, brought them closer together, albeit by letter, and it was something he'd cherished.

All of that had ended when Margaret left. Although Philip had never referred to the separation, the sudden coolness of his letters made it clear he knew and was taking it badly. And somehow, he couldn't quite find the way to bring the subject up when writing to Philip, so he avoided any reference to Margaret altogether. Eventually he found he was only writing about station life, as if that was all his life amounted to, which of course, on one level, was true.

After reading Philip's letters he now felt frustrated and full of self-loathing, and in some indefinable way, diminished. He no longer looked forward to reading them. They would sometimes be left on the table for several days until he was in the right mood to face them, and it took a long time for him to write a reply.

The last one had sat there for three weeks, unopened.

RAF Station S-------
Nottinghamshire
September 31st, 1943

Dearest Mum and Dad,

Aren't you lucky to be getting these letters all at once (when I finally get round to posting them, that is). I imagine you both sitting down at the table in the parlour with a large pot of tea and a slice of Mum's fruitcake as you read them together. I am writing this sitting on the grass on the morning of what will be my first flight with my new crew, with our Lancaster providing a dramatic backdrop! Let me introduce my crew to you:

My pilot Tony, a Sergeant like me, is from Devon. He's rather quiet and unassuming, not at all like the instructors we had at OTU, and certainly not what I expected our Skipper to be. But I like him, and feel confident in his company, and I'm sure he will do his level best to keep us all safe, as well as doing his job to help win the war. He is fond of dogs, and we had a right old time comparing notes about Meg and his collie, who is called Elsie. He has flown four operations over Germany, although he hasn't told me too much about them so far.

Our bomb aimer is a Taff, from some place that is all L's and Y's and completely unpronounceable. I haven't quite got the measure of him, he's a bit moody and keeps himself to himself I feel. Doesn't like dogs, doesn't like fishing, doesn't like anything it seems except dropping bombs on Germans, which is fair enough I suppose, as that's his job!

Merv, our flight engineer, is from Australia, where his family have a sheep farm, and he regales anyone who will listen with stories of Life in the Outback, Kangaroos and so on. Hank, our trusty wireless op, is also a colonial, this time a Canadian. He worked in insurance in Winnipeg before volunteering.

Arthur, our navigator, is actually the highest-ranking member of the crew – he's a flying officer, but it's accepted that the Skipper, although an NCO, is the boss. Arthur's the old man of the crew, being 24, and from Staffordshire. He's also the only married man among us, and everyone instinctively looks up to him as 'The Wise One'.

Which leaves only the rear gunner, because I am to be the crew's mid-upper gunner! Our Tail-End Charlie is another northerner, but of the White Rose variety, from Rotherham. Don't worry Dad, we had a good laugh immediately, seeming to hit it off despite our rivalry, and we are already firm friends...

So now you've met my crew, and I think you'll agree they're a grand bunch. I didn't need to feel nervous after all, because the fellows were all extremely friendly and welcoming, and we spent the whole of last evening together, exchanging stories and generally getting on famously.

Well, I'd better sign off as there is so much to do today. I PROMISE to post these letters tomorrow and look forward to hearing all your news.

Lots of love,
Harry xxxx

After talking to the MO, he had stepped out of the SSQ into the late September sunshine, feeling rather light-headed. The shock, he supposed. Adrenalin.

All around him airmen and ground crew, administrative officers and WAAFs scurried about like ants, each doing his or her bit for the war effort. He saluted passing colleagues automatically, so absorbed was he in his inner dialogue. Perhaps the doc was right, and he should go back into the retirement the RAF had called him out of four years ago. He'd be dead within a matter of months, maybe less, so what was the point of carrying on here? What was the point of any of it, really?

But he knew he couldn't go home to that empty house, not to die. For a while he seriously thought about writing to Margaret and telling her about the diagnosis, but he feared that she would think he was trying to get her to come back, or worse, just feeling sorry for himself. But he would have to tell her that he was dying, in the end, wouldn't he? And Philip deserved to know the truth as well.

The rest of the day passed uneventfully. Mercifully, he found that having work to do stopped him from thinking. At lunch in the Mess, he'd listened to some chaps discussing a show they'd seen in Lincoln, but didn't mention his visit to the MO when somebody remarked that he looked as if he had something on his mind. Hobson, the WAAF who brought him his three o'clock cup of tea, said that the Met Officer had whispered that the forecast looked promising for the next 36 hours, usually code for 'the squadron is on ops tomorrow night'. This meant he would spend the rest of today and tomorrow attending to mountains of paperwork, taking letters or memos from a tray marked IN on one side of his desk, and later placing them in a tray marked OUT on the other side. Towards six he heard Hobson humming to herself as she typed, and was about to tell her to keep it down a bit when he thought he recognised the tune.

'What's that you're humming, Hobson?' he asked.

'Sorry sir, I didn't mean to disturb you.'

'No, that's alright. But what is it?'

'The Thingummybob Song, I think. Well, that's what I call it anyhow. Gracie Fields sings it. She's the girl that makes the thing that drills the ...something that somethings something that's going to win the war.' She laughed. 'I've a frightful memory, sir.'

He didn't say anything, and Hobson got on with her work. She glanced over at him a few times, and saw that he hadn't moved, still staring into space. She almost jumped when he scraped back the chair and stood, saying he was going out.

'When will you be back, sir?' she asked.

But he had already gone.

'The usual, duck?'

The barmaid had seen him as he came into the bar and was already holding a bottle of his preferred whisky.

'You know me too well, Connie,' he said, and leant against the bar, one foot resting on the polished brass foot-rail running around the perimeter.

'Well, that's a turn up for the book,' she said, measuring the whisky.

'What is?'

'You've never called me Connie before.'

'Haven't I? Well, I've heard one or two of the other regulars and um...' He paused. 'I hope you don't mind me calling you Connie.'

'Course not, duck. It's me name, in't it?'

She brought the glass over and set it on the bar in front of him.

'So?' she said.

'So what?'

'So what's your name? I can't just call you Squadron Leader, can I?' She leant in, mischievously. 'Or is it an Official Secret?'

He stared at her for a moment, before smiling. 'Squadron Leader Ronald Emerson, Retired. But my friends call me Ronnie.'

'Thank you, Ronnie.'

He raised the glass and knocked the whisky back in one, grimaced, and started coughing.

'Not getting any better, is it?' she said.

'Another please, Connie,' he wheezed. 'Make it a double.'

'A double – at the double, sir!' She saluted and went back to the spirits, laughing at her own joke.

He paid for the drinks and inwardly relaxed, the confusing thoughts that had been whirling around in his head seeming to calm and settle now he was in the familiar, safe surroundings of the pub.

'Bad day?' she asked, gently. He smiled and shook his head.

'I'm fine, thanks.'

'This place feels a bit more like home, eh duck? Bit o' company and a nice warm fire.'

'Yes, something like that.'

'Chance to get away from the wife too, I wouldn't wonder.'

After a few moments during which an awkward silence hung over them, Connie moved off. He knew that although respectful of the social distance between them and not wanting to overstep the boundaries of her profession, she had been encouraging him to talk. But there was no way on God's earth that he was ever going to discuss personal matters with a barmaid. He just wasn't that sort of chap. Getting On With It had been drilled into him since school. Once, he'd actually broken his wrist in a cricket match and batted on until he passed out from the pain, and for a time he'd been the hero of the Second XI. And besides, pleasant and professional as Connie seemed, could he really trust her not to blab all his intimate secrets around town?

He was still standing at the bar, deep in his own thoughts, when they came in; a bunch of airmen, quite likely a crew from the station, although he didn't recognise any of them. Hardly surprising, given the numbers who passed through the squadron these days. One of the lads, an air gunner, was evidently a new member of the crew. They introduced him to Connie, who told him not to believe anything they said about her, and his laugh sounded a little too forced. A couple of glances from the other members of the crew confirmed that they had seen him at the far end of the bar, and almost imperceptibly they shifted their positions so that none except the new boy was looking in his direction.

Something else he had become used to, these days... Absorbed in his private thoughts, he returned to staring at his glass and slowly swirled the amber liquid around.

This much at least he knew; he didn't fear death, that was something he had become all too familiar with in recent months. But he was afraid of dying alone. Until recently it had never been something he'd even considered; now he worried that one day they would kick the door down and find him dead in his bed, after he had failed to turn up for morning briefing two or three days on the trot. Or he feared that his condition would worsen so much that he would be carted into a hospital to die, alone, and unmissed...

'Excuse me, sir... sir?'

He looked up and saw a young airman, pint glass in hand.

'Me and the lads are having a few drinks in memory of... well, we're having a bit of a celebration if you like, and I wondered if I could buy you a drink, sir, as you seem to be alone?'

It was the boy who'd come in earlier with his crew. He glanced over the boy's shoulder, to the group of airmen standing at the bar, pints and cigarettes in hand, ruddy faced, Brylcreemed, glaring at him with barely disguised contempt.

'Thank you, sergeant,' he said. 'That's a very kind offer, but I think your friends might have other ideas.'

The boy's expression changed. 'Are you sure you're alright, sir?'

He looked at the boy for a moment, remembering Philip, probably no more than two years older than this one, and was about to speak when a hand appeared on the boy's shoulder and a sergeant pilot interrupted: 'I'm sorry, sir, he's new to the squadron, and doesn't know the form. I'm sure the chairman of the committee wouldn't want to dirty his hands by drinking with us flying types. Come on, Bumfluff.'

The pilot tried to pull the boy away, but he resisted, standing his ground.

'I beg your pardon, sir. I didn't mean to be rude. I just

thought you looked like you could do with a bit of company, that's all. Sorry, sir.'

And before he could say anything, the two airmen had re-joined the group, and stood with their backs to him.

His cheeks burned. Eyes stinging, he took a minute to compose himself, downed what was left of his whisky, grabbed his greatcoat and cap, said 'Night, Connie,' and walked out of the bar and into the market square. He almost collided with a group of airmen, who had formed a short pyramid with one drunken soul on top, reaching up to tie a scarf around the head of the Saracen, which already sported a pair of flying goggles. An airman apologised, another swore, and the pyramid collapsed noisily, and he turned the corner, navigating his way through the dark, narrow backstreets.

Usually, he would catch a bus from the station by the Cross, but tonight he just carried on walking, his hands thrust deep into his greatcoat pocket, collar pulled up against the chill of the clear, starry night. As he passed through the outskirts of the blacked-out town, his footsteps echoing in the silence, the road was illuminated brilliantly by the moon, almost full, hanging high in the starry blackness of the night. He walked a slightly zig-zag path, the effects of the whisky thankfully anaesthetising the desperation that was steadily consuming him.

The walk home took over an hour, and he didn't meet a soul, barely even aware of the last bus from town as it sped past him. As he lifted the latch on the garden gate, he stopped and looked at the cottage, still and dark. He seemed to be seeing it for the first time, which in a sense he was, having never stood in the moonlight gazing at it as he did now. How had he never done that before? he wondered. What a waste. It was such a beautiful little house, and he'd never really appreciated it. He thought he heard the distant drone of aircraft engines, and standing half-way up the path, he looked up into the black, starry sky, craning his neck back until he could look no higher. Mouth open, his breath rising in clouds, he stood there, looking for something, and seeing nothing.

The next morning, half an hour before dawn, the silence was broken by the metallic grinding of the great hangar doors being pushed open. A tractor coughed, spluttered and slowly pulled P-Popsie, like some enormous black prehistoric bird, out onto the airfield.

Chiefy Bennett had kept the ground crew working on her through the night, in anticipation of this evening's operation; the station commander, keen not to antagonise Group[6] without good reason, expected all aircraft to be serviceable for what was going to be a Big Show. The fitters had been crawling all over her, repairing damage from the night fighter attack that had necessitated the replacement of the mid-upper gunner a few nights ago; replacing shattered Perspex turret panels, tracing and fixing sheared cables, repatching aluminium skin, and generally working to get the Lancaster 'On The Top Line'. Now he needed P-Popsie out at her dispersal point, so his team of flight mechanics could do the final repairs on the engines, at least one of which had sustained cannon-fire damage during the attack.

Despite not having fallen into bed much before one o'clock, the crew of P-Popsie were woken around the same early hour by a service policeman, doing his rounds with a clipboard and torch, and after going through the motions of washing and dressing they stumbled their bleary way to breakfast. Wherever they were going tonight, the crews knew that they had a full day's work ahead of them. Checks, briefings and night flying tests all before lunch, then there would be the Grand Reveal of the Target for Tonight, followed by yet more briefings and more checks, before take-off at dusk. If all went well and they returned, there would be de-briefings and their throbbing heads probably wouldn't hit the pillow before four o'clock in the morning.

After breakfast, during which little was said and copious amounts of tea were drunk, and still nursing a thick head, air

---

[6] For the purposes of organisation, Bomber Command was divided into Groups. If the station in this story was actually Syerston, it would be part of 5 Group.

gunner Harry Greenhalgh strolled across the airfield, surprised to see the tremendous amount of activity already taking place. He asked a passing erk[7] if he knew where to find P-Popsie, and followed the man's grunted directions, heading to a dispersal point out on the perimeter where he eventually found a Lancaster surrounded by bicycles, stepladders and toolboxes. Engine cowling panels lay on the ground, and fitters crawled over her upper surfaces, reaching into her inner recesses, straining and swearing as they tried to finish the job before the canteen closed for breakfast. Moving closer, he could make out the large dark red squadron codes and the letter P, indicating his aircraft. He nodded shyly at the ground crew as they clocked him, walking under the great bird's wings, until he was standing below the mid-upper turret, where a couple of armourers were discussing the finer points of football as they fed long belts of .303 ammunition into trays.

This would be his office tonight.

Later that morning, fully kitted up, the crew of P-Popsie sprawled on the grass a few yards from their Lancaster, waiting for Chiefy to pronounce her serviceable and ready to fly.

Not much was said. Someone read a copy of the *Daily Mirror*, a couple played cards, and another lay on his back, hands behind his head, looking up into the sky, watching the clouds change shape and imagining what his new baby daughter must look like now. Eventually Chiefy approached from the Lancaster, Form A700 in hand, pronouncing P-Popsie fit and healthy for her Night Flying Test. As the crew rose up from the grass, Harry was about to put the letter he'd been writing into his pocket when he had a thought; he called a fitter over, asking if he wouldn't mind taking the letter back to his billet and leaving it on his bed, ready for posting later. The fitter promised he would and hurried on to catch up with his mates.

---

[7] 'erk' – RAF slang; originally 'airk' (short for Aircraftman), meaning a person of low rank.

The crew climbed into the aircraft and prepared to put P-Popsie through her paces. In the mid-upper turret, Harry dug deep into his flying suit pocket and found his lucky rabbit's foot keyring, bought on holiday in Filey, relieved that he hadn't left it in his room. Shortly after eleven, the Skipper started up the Merlins, ran them for a few minutes to check for mag drop, and when he was satisfied the Lancaster rolled forward, turned onto the runway and took off into the air.

The unladen bomber lifted easily into the sky, and whilst still climbing, the Skipper started a sharp banking turn to the left. Behind his guns, Harry couldn't help smiling as the horizon tilted at a crazy angle and he saw the silver ribbon of the Trent thread its way through the Nottinghamshire landscape below him. He watched a green toy bus move slowly along a straight road and pass a group of red-brick cottages. The Lancaster was still low enough for him to see a figure emerging from the front door of one of the cottages and look up.

From his position a hundred feet beneath the bomber, Ronnie Emerson didn't see Harry. He was looking at a stream of oily, black smoke pouring from the Lancaster's starboard outer engine, hearing the loud and distinct bangs as first its propellor, and then the starboard inner's stuttered and stopped. The huge black aircraft suddenly dipped, as if caught by a powerful hand that flipped it over and hurled it downwards. The remaining two Merlins screamed as the Lancaster arrowed vertically towards the earth, and disappeared behind a wood. There was an awful crump; a shower of spinning fragments flew up and a huge orange fireball erupted as the fuel tanks on P-Popsie exploded, followed by a mushroom of black smoke, billowing into the sky.

It was all over in seconds.

He would find it hard to remember the exact sequence of events following the crash, but vivid images and details of what happened over the next few hours burned themselves indelibly into his brain: running along the road towards the burning wreck, the searing pain in his lungs, finding a gate (locked – damn!) climbing over it and running across the corn stubble towards the burning Lancaster; the sudden, unexpected heat of the flames, smoke stinging his eyes, the acrid smell of fuel and burning metal and flesh, the alarm bell of the fire tender hurtling up the Fosse.

It all ran through his brain like fragmented images in a nightmarish film: the roar of flames, the slowly-emerging skeleton of the Lancaster as the fire ate away at its metal skin; the crack of ammunition going off in the heat; men shouting as they dragged fire extinguishers and hoses across the field; the sudden quiet as the flames were smothered by high-pressure foam so that he now became aware of the chatter of people, pouring out of a green bus; a red-faced service policeman drawing his revolver and yelling at them to get back; the hacking at metal and Perspex with axes, the pulling of bodies, largely unrecognisable as such, from the smoking wreckage, to be placed on stretchers or tarpaulins and carried to the blood wagon. And later, once all the locals and dogs had been cleared away, the issuing of sacks and cricket-stump length poles with nails in the end, and the sight of erks wandering the field in lines, collecting small body parts; a man in overalls, sitting at the edge of the field, his head in his hands, wiping away tears; identity tags collected and laid on the bonnet of the station commander's staff car; serial numbers matched and ticked off a list; somebody saying 'Seven. That's the lot then.'

Within a few hours the carcass of the Lancaster had been winched aboard a Queen Mary Trailer and carried away. The Home Guard posted sentries, watching for children on the look-out for unexploded ammunition. The staff cars and trucks pulled away. There would be no investigation, no inquiry. It was an accident, just one of those things that happen in wartime.

On the large wall-sized blackboard in the Watch Office,

the line containing the details of P-Popsie and her crew was wiped clean by a WAAF, and a back-up aircraft and scratch crew was quickly thrown together in order to ensure the squadron maintained its strength for the night's big effort over Germany. And although every crew on the station was aware of the incident, there was little time to dwell on it. They attended briefings, groaned and swore as the target was revealed, went over routes and weather reports, and checked fuel and bombloads; letters were written, flying kits were donned, last cigarettes smoked and bladders emptied on tailwheels for good luck. As the sun set, the first of the Lancasters took off, and thirty minutes later both A and B Flights were in the air.

That was when the committee's work began.

As 'chairman', it was Squadron Leader Emerson's job to assemble the members of the Committee of Adjustment in his office: the station warrant officer, the padre, a sergeant clerk from the pay office and two trusted orderlies were given a list of the names of the seven airmen killed in the accident.

A truck pulled up outside the barracks, and the men of the committee went through the rooms, identifying beds. Quickly and quietly, they stripped the beds of their linen, piled it into bags for the station laundry and placed neatly folded fresh sheets and blankets on the bare mattress pads. They emptied lockers and cabinets of personal belongings, examining every pocket and wallet for photographs or any other evidence that might betray an affair, and searching toilet bags for prophylactics. Anything that might prove embarrassing, tokens of sexual conquests such as stockings or garters, along with rubbish including books and magazines, were thrown away or left for the surviving crews to divvy up; the rest was packed into boxes for return to the dead men's families. Flying kit and uniforms were returned to the stores to be re-issued.

Little was said during the process, other than the occasional response to a short question: 'Yes? No?' Often a shake of the head or a shrug would do. The members of the committee carried out their tasks dispassionately, and largely without emotion. The letter left on Harry's bed by a fitter that morning was thrown casually into a cardboard box along with the other letters, his pen, shaving kit, cufflinks and a handful of photographs.

When everything of interest had been removed, the squadron leader ran an expert eye over the beds, lockers, cabinets and surrounding walls. If all was clear, the committee could move onto the next billet and the whole process was repeated. This operation was carried out after almost every raid; as soon as it was known which crews had failed to return, even as the exhausted surviving crews were sleeping in nearby beds, the committee would go to work. If they did their job well, by the time the crews woke the next day, no trace of their former comrades' existence would remain, and replacement crews would never suspect that they were going to sleep in dead men's beds.

By mid-evening, with the operation over Germany still in progress, the Committee of Adjustment broke up, keen to get back to other jobs, or to the NAAFI in time for a sandwich, a mug of tea and a smoke. For some it would also be an opportunity to catch up on any station gossip and speculate on the possible cause of the crash.

He always reserved the task of vetting personal letters for himself. It wasn't a job that could be rushed or delayed; it demanded concentration and sensitivity if it was to be done properly. He saw it as his duty to ensure that, where humanly possible, any letters that would provide comfort to the bereaved, and not cause distress, or reveal military or romantic secrets, should be returned to the family. But he also understood that not everyone could read a letter, appreciating the subtle nuances, the sub-texts and the tricks that could betray a clue, a feeling, or a secret. It took a writer of letters to be a reader of them, and, at least until recently, he had considered himself more than up to the task.

When the committee had dispersed, he settled himself

in his office to read through the small pile of letters which had been left behind by the crew of P-Popsie. At first glance they did not seem to have been a particularly literary bunch. The pilot had left just a single letter, a communication from his brother Reg, who bemoaned the war's curtailment of his beloved pigeon racing. Harmless; he put it to one side for forwarding. More interesting were the half a dozen or so postcards that were in the bomb aimer's box. Evidently, he had a habit of instigating and maintaining intimate relationships with women in various parts of the country, each of whom appeared to believe that they were the sole objects of the man's affections. These went into the bin. The navigator had a small bundle of letters, all extremely short, from his wife in Rugely, all variations on the 'Dear Arthur, thank you for your letter, I am glad that you are well, the baby is well, I am doing well, all things considered...' theme. Nothing of interest or concern there, safe to be returned. The rear gunner, wireless operator and flight engineer had left no letters. He had long ago stopped wondering how this could be so.

He lit a cigarette and stretched, exhausted by the events of the day, his nerves already shredded. In front of him sat the small pile of rather thick-looking envelopes, sealed and addressed letters which the mid-upper gunner had evidently written but not posted. He picked one up and turned it over between his fingers, feeling its thickness and weight. The boy must have had a lot to write home about. They would take some time to go through if he was going to do the job properly.

He dropped the letter and was rubbing the tiredness out of his eyes and trying to hold off the rising wave of despair that seemed determined to overwhelm him, when he stopped; through the open window, probably from the wireless on the NAAFI van, came the sound of the popular song that Hobson had been singing yesterday.

Hearing the song properly for the first time he smiled, appreciating the cleverness of the lyrics. War was like a machine, that was a cliché, but the song took the cliché to another level, laughing at the absurdities of total war, at the same time acting as a recruiting sergeant to get more workers into the factories. It occurred to him for the first time that this was what war amounted to, when it came down to it: it wasn't the men firing bullets at each other from trenches or raining phosphorous bombs on women and children from a great height. It was about which side had the capability to organise, pay for and execute the biggest and most expensive military operation. Dockets, warrants, invoices and orders; queried, approved, stamped and signed, IN/OUT. Was this what Goebbels meant by total war?

In his mind's eye he saw himself from above, sitting like some deranged clerk at a huge desk, surrounded by the flotsam and jetsam of young men's lives, poring over letters containing their most personal, intimate thoughts and expressions, each item to be forwarded on to a loved one if considered useful to the war effort, or incinerated if not, much like the young men themselves. War was a machine, pure and simple, and he, it had suddenly become clear, was as much a cog in that machine as the factory girl in the song and the boys climbing into their Lancasters every night.

The wave of despair that he had been holding back finally rose up to engulf him. Fearful of being heard or seen in this state, he fought to hold back the sobs, covering his mouth with the back of his hand, but it was no good. Soon he collapsed in a fit of uncontrollable coughing and tears.

After several minutes, he wiped his eyes, exhausted, and realised that his outburst must have gone unnoticed in the adjoining offices. He looked at the letters, and for a moment actually considered the possibility of burning them and walking away. After all, who would know? He flicked open his lighter, staring at the flame, and then closed it again. He knew he couldn't destroy them arbitrarily; the lad had written them, they had to be read. But he couldn't do it here.

He put the envelopes into his pocket, switched off the desk lamp and headed out. If he was quick, he'd catch the next bus into town.

In the bar room of The Saracen's Head he had found a table in the corner, and sat down to read Sergeant Greenhalgh's letters. Connie, bless her, had interrupted him a few times, but she meant well, and soon he had read the first three, written to the boy's parents; the first covering his train journey from Scotland, and the others describing in some detail life on the station. The letters were warm, simple and honest, well-written and engaging. There were admittedly some unfortunate references to names and places which he was easily able to redact with his pen, but all in all he couldn't see how they would bring anything but comfort to the lad's parents.

He slit open the last envelope, addressed to a WAAF at a station in Scotland, and clearly, unlike the others, written in haste.

RAF Station S-------

My darling Anne,

It's gone two in the morning, I can't sleep, and am writing this on my knee in the ablutions so as not to wake the other fellows. I have to confess to getting filthy drunk this evening so this letter probably won't make much sense and will likely come across all gushing and Over The Top, but you know you really are the most important person in the world to me, and I need to tell you these things, if only because I hope you may understand just a little bit of what I am trying to say. Please don't screw this up. Not yet anyway.

It seems like it took days to get here on the train (air raids, diversions and what-not) and all the time me thinking about our precious night together, and the damnable argument that happened the next morning. As I looked miserably out of the window on the bus which took me the last few miles to the aerodrome, I noticed the most beautiful little cottages dotted along the road, and I couldn't help thinking that maybe one day when this is all over (or perhaps even before then?) we might be able to find a little place like that to rent, where we could be happy in each other's company, sitting beside a roaring fire in the winter, tending the garden in the spring and summer, or just sharing a bed, just the two of us, alone together, to live as we want to, without a care in the world, NO WAR and with nothing but a happy future together to occupy our thoughts.

And it suddenly hit me that although I always thought being able to fly was the most important thing to me, I realised that there is one thing more important, and that is you, darling Anne, and the love I have for you. If only we can forget the hateful things that were said, and which I am sure neither of us truly meant, we can find a way out of this awful mess.

Do I sound like I've had too much to drink? I hope not. You mustn't think this is just the beer talking. It's just that although I am happy beyond words to be finally in a place where I can do my bit in the war, I am going to be so far away from you. I can honestly say that suddenly having all this distance between us for the first time I now see clearly how much you mean to me (please, PLEASE don't throw this away, I beg you!)

The rest of the letter was written in a neater, less rambling hand, and was separated from the first section by the underlined words:

An hour later.

Anne, I realised I was sounding like Leslie Howard on a bad day, and made myself a VERY STRONG mug of coffee, and smoked two cigarettes outside, which has helped clear my head somewhat. I did a fair bit of thinking too and shall endeavour to ensure that the remainder of this letter reads like it has been written by a man of sound mind, low blood-alcohol level, and a Happy Heart.

The aerodrome is a splendid place, all very new and comfortable, and VERY BIG! After I'd drawn my kit etc and found a billet I was feeling a bit lonely, wondering when I would meet my crew, and I was half-way through writing a letter to my parents when I was scooped up (literally) by two Hairy Colonials and frog-marched off to the crew room, where I found my new crew, lounging about in their armchairs.

'Here's the sprog,' said Hank, one of the Hairy Colonials, and I was suddenly aware of six pairs of eyes, all looking me over, taking the measure of me. It was rather unnerving, I must say. I felt like a beast at market, pushed into the auction ring and forced to parade up and down under the scrutiny of cold, experienced eyes. Would I be good enough for this crew, would I fit in?

'About time,' announced one fellow, throwing down his newspaper. 'We thought you were lost. Good job you're not our new bloody navigator.' (General laughter). Without getting up he introduced himself as 'The Skipper' and told me that P-Popsie was 'in urgent need of a new mid-upper gunner, owing to the last one not being as alive as he used to be, thanks to a scrap with a night fighter over Essen a couple of nights ago.'

I was a little surprised, not realising that I was to be a replacement for a dead man. I suppose I had just assumed that I was to be part of a new crew. Registering my confusion, the Skipper told me not to worry, the turret had been hosed out and wiped down by the erks and was spick and span, so you'd never know.

He said this with an absolutely straight face, and there was a deathly silence as I took it in. I half-expected the crew to burst out laughing at the joke, but no-one moved. They all looked awkward, as if no-one knew what to say. 'I'm sorry to hear that,' I said, finally. 'You must miss him terribly.'

'Of course,' said the Skipper. 'Old Wilko was a bloody good bloke.' (Nodding in agreement). 'More importantly though, before we took off he had the foresight to pay me back the five quid he owed me, and he said that on no account must I use the money for anything other than getting the lads thoroughly drunk if he didn't come back.' Several of the crew smiled at this. 'And on that happy note,' he continued, rising to his full height, 'seeing as it looks like we'll be on ops tomorrow night, we are all going to the Saracen's to get well and truly plastered. Bus leaves in ten minutes.'

At one point the bus passed through a small village, the name of which I remembered from my history lessons as the site of *a major battle of the Wars of the Roses.*[8] *I mentioned this to the wireless op, telling him that as far as I remembered, it was thought to have cost the lives of as many as six or seven thousand men. 'Can you imagine?' I continued, 'All those men killed in one day?'*

'I don't have to imagine,' he said. 'That's how many we kill every night when we hit those German cities.'

I have to say I was stunned by what he said, and equally by the way he said it; as if he were describing something casual, routine.

'There's a difference though,' Tail End Charlie piped up, from his seat behind us, not taking his eyes off the racing page of his newspaper. 'We're burning women and children, not just men.'

Do you think that could be true, Anne? Or was it just another one of this crew's very dark jokes? I couldn't get the thought out of my mind, at least until we hit the Saracen's.

The Saracen's Head is a rather large affair, an old coaching inn located slap bang in the middle of the marketplace, and it gets a very favourable mention in Sir Walter Scott's novel 'The Heart of Midlothian', apparently. There are plenty of pubs to choose from in the town, but the lads seem to like this one, with its rather imposing statue of a bearded Saracen above the door.

The Skipper slapped the five-pound note on the bar and told the barmaid to 'Keep the beers coming while there's a man still standing,' and the drinking began. I was a little surprised that nobody made any kind of a speech about Old Wilko, the fellow who was paying for the beer and who I am replacing, and kept expecting the speeches to come with each round, but somehow they never did. I think though, that the crew were all remembering him in their hearts and were maybe just a bit embarrassed to make a show of their feelings.

Half-way through the evening I noticed a rather elderly officer (a squadron leader, I think) who was drinking alone. He looked rather preoccupied and weighed down by his thoughts.

---

[8] Presumably East Stoke, site of the Battle of Stoke Field, 1487, less than two miles north of RAF Syerston on the Fosse Way.

Now my parents always brought me up to treat everyone I meet as my equal (or at least no better than me!), and so although I know it's not entirely the done thing for an NCO to talk to an officer, I headed over and asked if we could buy him a drink, in memory of my predecessor. Suddenly everything was silent and rather awkward, and the old chap looked at me as if he'd seen a ghost. The fellows glared at him like he was Blind Pugh – the way they acted I half expected him to hand one of them the Black Spot. The Skipper quickly intervened, saying that 'the Chairman of the Committee wouldn't want to drink with the likes of us flying types.' With that the Skipper turned his back on the poor old squadron leader, rather rudely I thought, and I last saw him heading out of the pub looking like his world had collapsed around him.

The letter continued for another couple of pages, mostly romantic stuff about how much the boy was missing his girl, who it appeared was several years older than him, and more hero-worship of his new crew. When he had finished reading it, he folded the pages, slid them back into the envelope, and threw it into the fire. He watched the flames lick around the edges of the envelope before finally consuming it, and when he was satisfied that the contents were completely burnt, he put on his greatcoat and cap and went out into the night.

Sitting on the bus as it headed down the Fosse Way, he looked out of the window, mentally listing the jobs that he would have to do that night. First, he would gather and pack all the personal effects and letters from P-Popsie's crew that were suitable for return to the families and forward them, with personal letters expressing his sympathy for their loss. This would include the unposted letters written by the air gunner to his parents. After that he would grab some food and wait for the return of the squadron's Lancasters from Germany, and if required, the Committee of Adjustment would begin its work again.

All this would be easy; he had done it a hundred times.

It would be harder to go back to the dark, empty cottage when these jobs were done, but he would do it. And once inside, he would open one last letter, and sitting at the table with a pot of tea, he would read it, before taking his pen and writing a reply.

A Different Angle

'A documentary film?'

The station commander peered through the brown paper strips that criss-crossed the panes of his office window, scanning his airfield. On this cold, dull morning all he could see was rain and a solid layer of low, grey cloud. There were no aircraft in the sky, only a few black shapes sitting miserably out at dispersal, and the windsock hung limply on the horizon beyond No 1 Hangar. A few figures, ground crew mostly, scurried across the concrete, hands thrust deep into greatcoat or overall pockets, collars up. Down below, a young WAAF stood in a doorway, a newspaper held over her head, trying to decide whether to make a dash for it.

'Can't see that you'll have anything particularly interesting to film here. Especially in this weather, Miss...' He turned to the small, bright-eyed woman sitting on the other side of his desk.

'Morgan. Ginny Morgan. But please call me Scotty, most people do.'

'...Scotty?'

She took a long drag on a roll-up and casually tapped the ash into her cupped hand. 'I can see you're trying to work out the connection between a Welsh surname and a Scottish nickname,' she said, in a voice that hinted at many long nights involving cigarettes and whisky; 'Well don't bother, because there is none. It's simply that people who know me well say I possess all the characteristics of a Scottish terrier – a fierce tenacity tempered by a beguiling loyalty. Once you get to know me, that is.'

She smiled, winningly, and the station commander leaned across the desk, holding out a tin ashtray, looted from a local pub. Scotty Morgan tipped the ash into it and slapped her hands clean. She was wearing several layers of woollen jumpers and cardigans beneath a workman's leather jacket, shapeless corduroy trousers and flat shoes – an ensemble that wouldn't have been out of place on the Parisian Barricades during the Commune. The knitted multi-coloured woollen beret set off the whole thrown-together look perfectly.

'We're not expecting to find glamour, thrills and excitement here, although I'm sure you have it in spades.' The young man who had been staring at the few framed photographs hanging on the office wall spoke for the first time, without, the station commander noted, actually turning to face them. 'Quite the opposite, in fact. This film is going to be about squadron life in all its mundane reality. We want to capture something of the day-to-day business of life on the base.'

'We prefer to call it a station. We're not American.'

'Of course. The station,' said the young man, finally turning to face the room. In his early twenties, he was a good thirty years younger than Scotty Morgan, slim and whey-faced, wearing a fawn military-issue duffle coat and the kind of beard that signified a bit too much of the intellectual for the station commander's liking.

'Of course, the film will reflect the dedication, commitment and sacrifice demanded by the war effort, from all of us. Wartime life, in all its humdrum ordinariness, but tied together by an understanding of what makes a bomber crew tick. A simple story that the audience can relate to, giving mothers and girlfriends a window, so to speak, through which to see the kind of lives their young heroes lead on the station. And vice versa – we won't be ignoring the WAAFs and the women who man the NAAFI wagon, as it were.' He couldn't resist smiling at his own joke.

'A simple story?' The station commander raised an eyebrow. 'If you're expecting any of my chaps to act you'll be on a hiding to nothing. The last Christmas show was an absolute shocker.'

Scotty Morgan smiled sweetly for the station commander, teeth hidden. 'Perhaps Jeremy is giving you the wrong impression. We are not here to make *One Of Our Aircraft Is Missing...*

'Thank God,' muttered the young man under his breath.

'...The Films Division of the Ministry of Information have commissioned us to make a short documentary piece, a slice of life if you like, no more than ten minutes long, that can sit comfortably between the newsreel and the main feature at the Essoldo, Reigate. That's all.'

The station commander noticed a frown fall over the young man's face, and turned back to the older woman. 'That all still sounds a bit vague, if you don't mind my saying. What is it that you are actually hoping to film?'

Scotty Morgan selected another roll-up from a small, battered tobacco tin and waved it theatrically in the air. 'Good point. Our working title is *A Day In The Life Of A Bomber Crew*. I'm the film's producer, Jeremy here is my director.

'Really? You're the director?' The whey-faced young man looked hardly old enough to watch a film, never mind make one, but then his bomber crews were mostly the same age, and they were doing a real job. 'Will I have seen any of your films? I pop into the station cinema as often as I can, work permitting.'

The young man looked down at his pale, thin hands. 'No. Actually this is my first time as a director.'

The station commander waited for him to continue but there was silence. Scotty Morgan picked up the baton.

'Jeremy joined the unit straight from Cambridge, and is brim-full of all kinds of exciting ideas. We're giving him his first opportunity as a director on this job, and are sure he's going to deliver, aren't you, lovey?'

Jeremy nodded. The station commander looked doubtful.

'You can rest assured that he and the crew will be in my safe hands throughout shoot, station...' She paused, and leaned forward in her chair, roll-up hanging on her lower lip: 'Look I'm sorry but I can't keep calling you "Station Commander", it sounds so frightfully militaristic.'

'Will Group Captain Connolly do?'

'Much better, thank you. And reassuringly alliterative.' Scotty Morgan sat back, and the young director smiled thinly, as if sharing an in-joke.

The station commander felt his cheeks burn. He could tell when the mickey was being taken, and he didn't like it, especially when the mickey-takers were civilians. Damned seagulls. They fly in, steal all the food, shit all over everyone and fly off again. No, it would be better all round if he just put paid to the whole ridiculous idea now. He was about to send them packing when his eye caught a piece of paper which Scotty Morgan had retrieved from the voluminous bag at her feet and was now unfolding for him.

'I'm so sorry, I forgot, they gave me this when I explained our idea to them at er... Group Headquarters? Everyone seemed to be entirely comfortable with what we were proposing and were sure you would have no objection. Quite the opposite, in fact, as you'll see.' She placed the crumpled letter on the desk. This was the other side of the Scottish terrier in full flow, the rat between her teeth, ready to break its neck with a simple tightening of the jaws.

The station commander read the letter quickly, his heart sinking, then stood and turned to look out of the window. The sun was struggling to break through a gap in the cloud and the rain was definitely easing. Down below he saw the young WAAF peer out from the doorway and decide to risk a dash along the path. Another normal day on the station, about to be disrupted by these clowns. Every instinct in his body was screaming at him to throw them out of his office now and forget that the whole ridiculous idea had ever been mentioned. But they were working for an official government unit. And they had authorisation – nay, enthusiastic approval, from Group.

He turned to face Scotty Morgan, who smiled at him, in what she obviously thought was her beguiling way, revealing dark, nicotine-stained teeth, challenging him to argue. She struck him as one of those women who knew how to get their way, even if it meant trampling all over someone like him.

'A day in the life you say? Well, just so long as you don't want to show my chaps in the evenings as well. Their mothers and girlfriends wouldn't want to see what they get up to in the local pubs and hostelries. Not a pretty sight, I can tell you.'

'Of course, we see your point, Group Captain Connolly. Considerations of taste will be as important to us as questions of security. The skill of a good documentary film maker is to remain invisible. If you are happy to let the crew get on with their jobs, I promise you won't even know we are here.'

The station commander sucked on the end of his moustache again. Scotty Morgan went in for the kill: 'Group were sure you wouldn't see a problem.'

'I suppose not,' he said finally, and despite the cold wave of unease rising up from his gut, he put the letter down on his desk. 'You'll have a week, no more. My adjutant, Squadron Leader Emerson, will be your point of contact – whatever you need he'll see to it.'

'Absolutely not. It's out of the question!'

Despite all the work happening around the Lancaster, the young pilot's words cut clearly through the noise, and heads lifted to see what the shouting was about.

'But the orders have come down from Group,' said Squadron Leader Emerson.

'I don't care if the orders have come down from God all-bloody mighty himself, I'm not having a bunch of long hairs buggering things up for my crew.'

Scotty Morgan glanced at the young director as he rolled his eyes wearily, and cut across him before he could say anything to make the situation worse.

'We really won't be any inconvenience to you, and we'll be out of your hair in just a few days.' She smiled her winning smile, but the pilot was having none of it.

'I don't mean to be rude miss, but I've never heard anything so ridiculous in my life. My lads don't want to be in a film. We're fighting this war, not playing at it.' He turned to the Squadron Leader. 'I'm sorry sir, if the station commander has a problem with that, I'll tell him the same thing to his face.' The pilot turned on his heel and strode towards the large black Lancaster sitting at dispersal where a small group of overalled fitters were standing, oily rags and tools in hand, watching with interest.

'Cross another one off the list,' said the young director, wandering off.

'Are all your pilots as independently minded as this?' asked Scotty Morgan.

'The good ones usually are,' the squadron leader replied, as laughter erupted from the group of men beneath the bomber, and they returned to their work. He thrust his hands into his pockets and sighed. Something had told him this wouldn't be easy when the station commander had dropped a crumpled letter into his in tray with the words, 'Do me a favour, Ronnie - find a crew to fob this lot off onto, there's a good chap. Can't stop, see you for lunch.' And this was the sixth crew he'd approached that morning. The negative responses were so immediate he began to suspect that word was getting around ahead of him.

'We seem to be getting nowhere fast, don't we?' he said, hoping to elicit some sympathy from Scotty Morgan. But her face wore an expression that clearly said *it's your job to find a crew to work with us, and we're going nowhere until you do.*

The squadron leader glanced over at the young director who was mooching around a few yards away, crouching down and peering at the Lancaster from the tail end.

'What's he doing?' he asked.

'Oh, don't mind Jeremy,' Scotty Morgan replied. 'He'll be planning shots, looking for different angles.'

'I see,' said the squadron leader, although he didn't quite. 'Look, why don't you and young Jeremy hang around for a few minutes and I'll have another word with this chap. He might see things differently once he's cooled down.'

'Oh, please don't bully the fellow on our account,' Scotty Morgan said, opening her tobacco tin. 'We don't want to cause a fuss.'

'Of course, but I might be able to pull a few strings.' He looked at the tin, containing a few roll-ups and a book of matches. 'By the way, it's not a good idea to smoke with all this aviation fuel around, not to mention the ammunition and bombs and so on. Wouldn't look good if you were to blow us all to Kingdom Come, eh?'

'Not unless the camera was rolling,' she laughed, revealing the nicotined teeth. 'Make quite a shot, eh?'

The squadron leader's face was impassive; irony was clearly not his strong point. 'Sorry, not funny,' she said. She pocketed the tin, watched as he strode over to the young pilot, then turned and found her director, who was still crouched down, behind the Lancaster, peering through a small circle made by his thumb and forefinger.

'Found any new angles?' she said.

'Down low, starting on the rear turret, shooting past the tail plane looks good. Slow dolly out – the bomber will look rather impressive in silhouette if Ziggy can get that.'

'Good,' she said. 'I'm sure he can. Assuming we even get that far.'

'I can't believe it,' he said, standing. 'Why is everyone so hostile towards us? Anyone would think we were the damned enemy.'

'To them we probably are.'

He looked at her. 'What do you mean?' She glanced over her shoulder, checking that their conversation was not overheard. 'Okay, our film, what's it about?'

'A day in the life of a bomber crew.'

'Well done, yes, that's the title - but the men in the film, the actual subjects of our little picture. What do they do?'

'You've seen the script, they'll be-'

'Forget your bloody script, Jeremy. I'm talking about reality. These men, who fly these bombers – what do they do?'

The young director played with his beard. 'Well, from what I've seen so far they seem to spend a lot of time lounging around and telling jokes. Plus they drink rather a lot.'

'Alright, let me rephrase it. That's what they *do*. But that's not what they *are*. What they are is Men Who Kill.'

He looked at her, unsure where this was going.

'Forget the lounging about, the jokes and the banter. Industrialised Mass Murder - that's the reality of what these men do, day in, day out, night after night. They fly over to Germany in their Lancasters and kill people; people they've never seen, and who, except possibly in a theoretical sense, they don't have any argument with. No wonder they get drunk and act the goat at the slightest opportunity.'

'I'm not sure what you're getting at,' he said.

'You really can be dense sometimes, Jeremy. Look, someone gets into an argument in the pub and punches you on the nose. Doesn't matter why, but you now have a personal beef with that man, and nobody would blame you if you punched him back, or even if one dark and rainy night you waited outside the pub for him to stagger out, and cracked a bottle over the back of his head. The beef is satisfied. Same goes for if a man steals from you, or sleeps with your wife. He does you wrong, you wrong him back, and if a bobby pinches you, well you'll be up before the magistrate but, and this is the important thing, you certainly won't be treated like a hero, nor would you expect to be.'

She had his full attention now. 'Go on...'

Scotty Morgan checked over her shoulder again. 'But that's not the case with these young men. The people they kill, on a regular basis and in large numbers, are, it could be argued, perfectly innocent. Yes, they are German, at least we expect most of them will be, and therefore they are The Enemy. But there a lot of foreign slave workers in those German factories, from Poland, Russia and France, and when you drop bombs on German factories you're going to kill a lot of people who are actually on our side. And that's not taking into account all the houses around the factories and the railway yards and the docks, houses occupied by ordinary German families, old people, children, and babies. Bombs don't ask questions and explode later. We all burn the same, Jeremy. Not a comfortable thought with which to lay your weary head on the pillow after a long and dangerous operation, is it, an operation in which, it has to be allowed, you may have personally cheated death by a hair's breadth and your best pal may not have been so lucky. Best forgotten, I'd say. Get in the bar, buy a round, laugh desperately at all the bad jokes, and do your best to tell yourself that what you were doing last night was morally justified, or just some awful dream, and that your bombs probably missed their target anyway. So everything's fine, or at least it appears to be. You keep your head down and hope you finish your tour. And then along we come, happily making a documentary film for the viewing pleasure and education of the massed millions on the home front, holding a mirror up to reality. *Their reality*. Not a mirror they particularly want to look in, is it, not a face they care to see staring back at them, do you see what I mean? So in that sense, and I apologise for going around the houses to reach my point, yes, we probably are the enemy, to them.'

'I must say, you sound like the enemy, when you talk like that, Scotty. I thought we were making a film about heroes, about men who were saving us from the tyranny of Fascism.'

'And so we are. But don't forget, however much you might think you're making *Citizen Kane*, this job is propaganda, pure and simple, and you better not forget it.'

Scotty Morgan turned, hearing the squadron leader's insistent cough. 'Any luck?'

From the look on the squadron leader's face, it was clear he'd not been able to pull any strings. 'We'll try S-Sugar,' he said. 'Len Walker's a decent type, might be able to persuade him to play ball. This way.'

But Len Walker didn't play ball, and neither did Piet de Jong, Sandy Lennox or Tommy Doyle or any of the others. None of the crews approached by Squadron Leader Emerson showed the slightest inclination to be involved in such a ridiculous stunt. And some put it more strongly than that. The squadron leader left the producer and director to wait for the expected arrival of their crew and equipment and joined the station commander in the Mess for lunch.

'*Nil desperandum*, Ronnie,' said the station commander, finding an empty table. 'I think you may be missing a trick here.'

'Really?' said the squadron leader. 'Well, I'd be grateful for the benefit of your wisdom. I'm stumped.'

The station commander sprinkled pepper over his sausage and mash. 'Quite sensibly you've put together a list of our best pilots and crews, the ones you know we can trust not to do something silly when they're bowled a googly by these damned film types. But actually, in refusing to be involved, it strikes me they are only demonstrating *why* they are the best.'

'What are you getting at?' asked the squadron leader. 'I thought they were just being rather arsey, if you don't mind my saying.'

'And so they were. Not eating? These bangers aren't bad.'

The squadron leader sighed. 'Not hungry.' He stifled the cough which had become worse over the last few weeks and which the station commander steadfastly refused to acknowledge, despite a recent word in his ear from the MO.

'Look,' said the station commander, 'a good crew doesn't manage to stay together for the number of ops some of these chaps have done by inviting danger, does it?'

'Danger?' Ronnie Emerson looked up. 'They're only making a short film about life on the station.'

'By taking unnecessary risks, I should have said, but it amounts to the same thing.' The station commander ate a forkful of sausage. 'These film people, by definition, are an Unknown Risk. Who knows, however well-meaning they are and how nicely they intend to behave, what tiny, unexpected things they might do or say that could upset the delicate balance of a good crew - sow the seeds of disharmony as it were, with just a misplaced comment or reaction. You know what it's like Ronnie, it's "one day in the life" to these film bods, but they are trespassing into that sacred magical union that is a bomber crew, men who live and die for each other on a daily basis. As an ex-pilot myself I can't say I'd be too happy if you were to ask me to put myself in that situation either.'

'Thank you, sir. If you remember, I didn't ask for the job.'

'I know Ronnie. I'm not blaming you, it's this film crew that is the problem. I knew they were trouble, the moment I clapped eyes on them, but we're stuck with them and their damned film whether we like it or not.'

'Well, what you say does make sense, I suppose.' The squadron leader took a sip of tea, and grimaced. 'But I still don't see how we are going to get out of this mess. I can't very well *order* a crew to take part. There'd be a riot.'

'Quite,' said the station commander. 'But there might just be a way...'

Ten days earlier the squadron had taken part in a raid on Turin. When the map was revealed at the briefing the crews had mostly breathed a sigh of relief that the long red string ended in northern Italy; the flak and fighter defences were likely to be much less onerous than for a German target, and flying over the Alps by moonlight was something you didn't get to do every day.

But the crew of Lancaster Q-Queenie never even saw those majestic moonlit peaks. A night fighter caught them on the way out over southern France, downing them with a single burst, the encounter witnessed by Len Walker's rear gunner. The aircraft exploded in mid-air; no 'chutes. It was the only loss suffered by the squadron that night, and not made any easier by the knowledge that Q-Queenie's crew, who had flown together for several months, were only three trips from completing their tour of thirty operations.

The replacement Lancaster had arrived at the station before its new crew; the big dark red letters were being painted on the black fuselage as the seven young men assembled, wide-eyed and nervous, in the crew room. Coming together from various Operational Training Units or nabbed as spares from nearby squadrons, they eyed each other warily, swapped stories and tried to look like they knew what they were doing. Their pilot, a sergeant from Gateshead named Keene, greeted each of his new crew with a firm handshake and a ready smile, and when the last man had arrived and they'd drunk tea and smoked cigarettes and dumped their bags in their billets, someone asked the question they had all been wanting to ask: when were they going to see their Lanc?

They found Q-Queenie on her hardstanding, a brand-new machine, looking and smelling factory fresh, and were quickly scrambling around inside it, finding their stations and imagining how it would feel on operations. They exchanged names with the ground crew, who already felt that the aircraft was theirs, to be loaned to the flyers on condition that they brought it back each night in one piece. They didn't notice the weary, cynical way in which the erks watched as they swarmed over their new toy, unconsciously judging how many ops it would be before this lot got the chop. At the current rate of losses, they were unlikely to get beyond four or five ops; four or five terrifying nights in which they would be blooded, in which to start to learn about themselves and their mates, who they could trust not to get them killed, and what they themselves had to do - or not do - if they wanted to survive to fly another night. If they learned quickly and were very lucky there was a chance – only a slim one, mind – that they might make it to the end of their tour. Not that they would be thinking about that. They soon learned that it was terrifying to even imagine flying thirty operations, and rationalised the fear by telling themselves it was bad luck to think about the end of the tour. Imagining still being alive at the end of the week was hard enough. It was easier to live for the moment, *in the moment*, to enjoy what you had while you had it. Don't even think about the next op; it will come soon enough and so long as you have your lucky charm with you…

'And you want these boys to be the crew in our film?' Scotty Morgan said from behind a cloud of cigarette smoke.

'Given the… logistical difficulties we've encountered in finding a crew who are actually willing to be filmed, the station commander thought the men of Q-Queenie would be an ideal choice.' The squadron leader turned to the young director, hunched on a chair. 'Don't you think? Jeremy?'

The young director blew his cheeks out. 'Well, it's not what we were thinking of. This film is supposed to depict a crew who are friends, comrades in arms, not a bunch of lads who don't know each other from Adam.'

'But who would know?' The words were no sooner out of his mouth than the squadron leader felt the full glare of the producer and director on him. 'I mean, they'll just be drinking cups of tea, reading the newspaper, sharing a joke with the NAAFI girls, won't they?'

'Have you read my script?' the young director demanded.

The squadron leader sighed. 'Not yet, I'm afraid. Been too busy finding you a crew.'

'What Jeremy is trying to say is that we are making a documentary film, which, if it is to enjoy any success must be realistic and believable. I fear it may be glaringly obvious to any audience if we are seen to be pretending that this is an experienced crew.'

'But will it? Really?'

'Yes, it will! *Really!*' The young director raised his voice for the first time, and Scotty Morgan noticed a petulant quality that she hadn't heard before but had always suspected might be lurking there.

The squadron leader came to his feet. 'Well, maybe this could work to our advantage,' he said. 'Tell me if I'm treading on any toes here but isn't there something rather interesting in showing our audience how a crew is formed? How the business of flying operations actually brings a group of men together into an efficient fighting unit?'

'Except that this bunch won't actually be flying operations over Germany this week, will they?' Again Scotty Morgan noted the worrying petulant tone.

'Possibly, possibly not – we won't know until it happens, so to speak, although theoretically at least they could be called on to fly operationally tomorrow night.'

'Before we get too carried away...' Scotty Morgan stubbed out her roll-up in a saucer, 'I think it only fair to remind us all that we will only be filming this crew because they are too green to understand the risk to their survival that we represent – according to Group Captain Connolly. Now whether it's actually true or not, are we comfortable with that fact?'

'I am sure that we can live with that,' said the squadron leader. 'If kept between ourselves, no one need lose any sleep about it.' The young director said nothing.

'Of course, the fact that none of these men will have flown operationally before will alter things, give the film a shift in perspective, a different weight so to speak, don't you think Jeremy?'

The young director looked up at Scotty Morgan, remembering their conversation that morning. Her face revealed nothing.

'And you have less than a week before the station commander wants you off his airfield,' said the squadron leader. 'Not a lot of time for deliberations.' The young director shifted his weight and ran a pale hand over his beard.

'Well, I suppose, with some rethinking and a few rewrites, I could make it work.'

The squadron leader smiled for the first time that day. 'Then I take it we are all happy?'

And so it was agreed. Squadron Leader Emerson suggested that in the absence of a new script they start shooting early next morning around Q-Queenie – he'd make sure it was ready for them at dispersal and see to it that the crew would be up bright and early. Borrowing a typewriter from Hobson, the squadron leader's WAAF secretary, (who also managed to scrounge a bottle of Scotch and a couple of packets of Luckies from the mess) the young director sat up all night, approaching the film from a different angle, sketching out a scenario which would tell the story of Q-Queenie's crew as they joined the squadron. As the whisky took effect and his imagination opened up, he rewrote the scenes and dialogue to show the new crew, awkward strangers at first, meeting, sharing stories that revealed their different backgrounds, seeing their aircraft for the first time, making friends with their ground crew, and laughing at jokes around the NAAFI wagon. A largely rewritten narration tied the new story together, and when Hobson entered her office at eight the next morning, she found the young director sprawled asleep in her chair, an empty bottle of whisky and an ashtray full of cigarette ends next to the new script.

'Well? What do you think?'

The young director sat next to Scotty Morgan in the canteen, trying to rub the dull ache of the hangover out of his temples.

'I think you look like shit,' she said.

'What do you think of the script?' he said. She put down her coffee.

'You want my honest opinion?'

'Of course.'

'It's shit. Unrealistic, dishonest, melodramatic, sentimental, cliched. Shall I go on?'

'But I was up all night writing it. I know it's not perfect but...'

'The one thing that comes across clearly is that you have absolutely no idea what you are writing about. This,' she flicked idly through the pages of the script, 'is a Cambridge graduate's romantic version of what it's like to be a fighting man in today's war. It's all fake.'

The young director's head felt as if it were about to explode, as the dull throb of the hangover was heightened by the sudden rise in his blood pressure. 'Hang on, Scotty. You never said that about the original script. And this is substantially the same – as you said, only the perspective has changed.'

'Yes, well the original script was shit as well. Unshootable.'

Jeremy struggled to make sense of what he was hearing. 'If it was unshootable, why were we going to shoot it?'

Scotty Morgan turned to look at the young director for the first time. 'Because those morons at the Ministry of *Dis*Information thought it was just what they wanted, and, more importantly, they were prepared to commission it. But honestly, they have no more idea than you do about how to make a realistic documentary film.'

'And you do, I suppose?'

'Yes, I do. You have seen the films I made about the women of the Clydebank shipyards in 1933? The mining community in the Rhondda in '35? The International Brigade in '36? I could go on...'

The young director felt sick. 'No, I haven't. I didn't -'

'Well, those were honest films, made by observing what was in front of my eyes and capturing it with the camera. I didn't write a script full of middle-class liberal claptrap about the deserving poor and expect my subjects to fit into it. I lived with them, watched them, learned about what they thought, how they felt, what made them laugh and cry, and then and only then did I dare to point my camera in their direction. They were the film, not some patronising nonsense in dialogue form.' The young director watched the light in Scotty Morgan's black eyes flash brightly as she remembered the old days. 'I had no idea what I was going to shoot, I didn't dare presume that I had some authority or control over the story, the story presented itself – my job was to find it, bring it together, and above all, to be respectful towards the people whose story it really was.'

Finished, she opened her tin and selected a roll-up. The young director held his head in his hands. 'Obviously I was not deserving of that same respect.'

'Don't sulk Jeremy, it's not a very endearing quality in a director. Grow up. Whatever you think, you're no Humphrey Jennings, nor ever will be, with that attitude.'

'So what am I doing here, if I'm so useless?'

'Better ask your mother, she pulled the strings to get you the job in the first place. Oh, don't get me wrong, you're a pleasant enough lad, not unintelligent, you've obviously got ambition and you're not afraid of hard work.' She tapped a finger on the script. 'But with my guidance and a lot of help from your crew you might just learn something about the job and become a halfway decent film maker.'

'Thanks, I suppose,' he said.

'You're welcome.' She blew a cloud of smoke into the air.

'I wish you'd said all this last night though, then I wouldn't have wasted all that time and have this blasted hangover.'

'It's all part of the learning process, dear boy. Finish your coffee.'

The young director drained his cup. 'So what are we going to do?'

'Well, we need to make the film, that's for certain, or nobody gets paid. In an ideal situation I would have thrown your script in the bin, told you to spend a few days living with your bomber crew and develop some sort of understanding of them before we started shooting as much footage as we could. Then we'd scurry away back down to Wardour Street, and I'd sort it all out for you in the edit. End result, we'd have a reasonably good film, the idiots at the Films Division wouldn't notice that it bore little if any relation to the thing they'd commissioned, you'd get your first credit, and we'd all be able to eat. But given that we are short on time and film stock, I think some level of improvisation is called for.'

The young director looked worried. 'Improvisation? That's not really my forte.'

Scotty Morgan smiled. 'Well, you'd better learn.'

An hour later the crew of Q-Queenie sauntered out to dispersal to find a film crew waiting by the Lancaster. Standing around between the huge lights on wheels, and a camera on a length of rail, were a good dozen or so people, who turned to acknowledge them. To one side stood the ground crew, watching with impassive faces, and there was an awkward silence before the lady in the baggy cardigans and beret stepped forward and introduced everyone.

'Everybody, say hello to Sergeants Keene, our pilot, and Armstrong, our flight engineer; to Flying Officer Wilson, navigator; Sergeant Bairstow, wireless operator; Flying Officer Dobson, bomb aimer; and our eagle-eyed rear and mid upper gunners, Sergeants Rankine and Harrison. No, that's the other way round – Harrison and Rankine!' There was immediate laughter. 'The crew of Q-Queenie and stars of our film.'

Everyone applauded as the airmen shifted embarrassedly, and then Scotty Morgan proceeded to name the film crew. 'This is Jeremy, our esteemed director, who we are extremely lucky to have on board; Ziggy, our director of photography and camera operator, currently on the run from occupied Czechoslovakia to where we hope he'll bugger off back soon; Gordon, who is recording sound – good luck with all these aeroplanes whizzing around; Jeanette who will be keeping an eye out for continuity; and our heroic chaps in the camera, sound and lighting departments who will no doubt be cadging cigarettes off you boys in blue over the course of the next few days, so watch out!'

There was a burst of laughter, and the atmosphere began to thaw, but Scotty Morgan was in full flow. 'I think we all know Squadron Leader Emerson, over by the tea urn, who is here to make sure we don't cause a security breach or blow anything up, and his assistant Corporal Hobson from the WAAF. Have I forgotten anyone?' There was a brief pause. 'Oh, yes, of course - *me* - Scotty Morgan, producer.' She beamed a huge smile and there was another burst of laughter as everyone fell for Scotty's mock humility. 'If anyone has any problems they should come and see me, and I'll point them in the opposite direction. Right, why don't we all get to know each other over tea and biscuits then we'll get to work. Lots to do, gang, lots to do!'

Led by their pilot, the airmen stepped forward, shaking hands, and laughing as they were handed mugs of tea. The squadron leader took Scotty to one side. 'That was impressive, I must say. How on earth do you remember all those names and jobs?'

'Preparation dear boy. It's not a big thing but it matters. And I find it shows respect.'

An hour and a half later, they hadn't shot anything. Jeremy was still trying to describe a complicated setup which he wanted to start with one gunner chatting to the other by the rear turret, the camera dollying out past the tailplane as a couple of the crew ran past throwing a cricket ball to each other, and finally picking up the pilot stepping out of the rear door to discuss the weather for tonight's raid with the navigator and bomb aimer. There was, to his mind, 'something heroic and yet restrained about the juxtaposition of the casual ball play with the ominous presence of the Lancaster looming behind them, a reminder of the reason they were here.' The bomber crew looked at him with mute incomprehension, and Scotty Morgan watched patiently as the young director then explained his idea to Ziggy, lights were eventually positioned, the camera set up, and Jeremy rehearsed the moves with the airmen.

'No, no, no, you still don't look natural,' he shouted, watching the airmen's wooden attitudes after the fifth rehearsal. 'You need to be more relaxed.'

'I don't feel relaxed,' said the wireless op, in a broad Liverpool accent. 'I feel like a twerp.'

The ground crew shared amused looks: this was going to be fun. Half an hour later, when with each painful rehearsal things were only looking even more hopeless, the young director turned to his camera operator.

'What do you think Ziggy?'

The older man thought for a long time, staring into the middle distance, then shrugged.

'It's your shot.'

The young director had no idea what that meant. It was everything he could do not to throw up or run away.

'Jeremy, we really should turn over,' Scotty Morgan called, looking at the sky. 'Time's winged chariot and all that.'

'Alright,' he said, trying to control the note of fear in his voice. 'First positions.' He caught a glimpse of the young WAAF, Hobson, standing with the squadron leader. She waved and gave him a quick fingers crossed. This was it.

He called his first 'Action!', and exactly forty-three seconds later, his first 'Cut.' The airmen relaxed, and everybody turned to the young director, waiting for his response.

Standing over his shoulder, Scotty Morgan said 'Well?'

The young director lowered his voice. 'Christ, that was awful. It was wooden, the chaps with the cricket ball missed their cue, and in the final grouping I could swear the bloody bomb aimer was looking directly at the camera...'

'Fine,' said Scotty Morgan. 'Check the gate!'

'Gate's clear,' said Ziggy, a little too quickly.

'Perfect! Well done everybody, we're moving on!'

There was a chorus of cheers and back-slapping among the airmen. Jeremy turned to see the squadron leader applauding enthusiastically, and the young WAAF gave him a thumbs up.

Jeremy found Scotty Morgan with Ziggy at the camera.

'Scotty, that was dreadful, worse than any of the rehearsals.'

'And it's not going to get any better, but we can't go wasting stock on extra takes. That's life, lovey.'

'But -'

'We're moving on Jeremy. Right Ziggy, what do you think?'

The older man moved quickly, suddenly animated. 'Let's get the boys in a group, over here, having a smoke, knock off a wide and some close ups, and then I'll get some of the plane.'

In the space of only a few minutes Ziggy and Scotty 'knocked off' a dozen brief shots of the crew around Q-Queenie, each of which had energy and a natural feel. Each shot was done with a minimum of rehearsal, with just a word or two of encouragement from Scotty, and in one take. The crew looked nervous but relaxed, which is what they were. At one point Scotty Morgan noticed the ground crew sniggering at the boys 'pretending to be war heroes' and called them over to join in. They declined her offer, but Scotty was having no nonsense, bringing both groups together and telling the ground crew to carry on winding up the flyers.

'What do we say?' asked one of the erks.

'Tell them what you'll do to them if they break your aeroplane!' The two groups laughed, the camera rolled, and the young director watched as Scotty Morgan worked her magic, effortlessly. Everyone was working efficiently and happily, material was being shot. It was all working.

'This is all tremendous fun, I must say.'

Jeremy was immediately taken by the striking blue of the young WAAF's eyes, which he hadn't noticed before. It was a cliché, he knew, but they definitely seemed to be enhanced by the blue of her uniform. 'Must be all rather old hat to you I know, but this is my first time on an actual film set.'

The WAAF had approached Jeremy who was sitting alone, in the canteen, staring at his script, desperately trying to make his brain work. The morning's shoot had been a painful – traumatic even – baptism of fire, as he had had to stand back and watch Scotty Morgan effectively do his job for him.

'Yes, it's er... interesting working in these conditions,' he said.

There was a beat when she could have walked away, but didn't. 'Do you mind if I join you? I couldn't help noticing you were alone. Unless I'm interrupting your work?'

'No, no, just going over shots. But I'm done. Please.'

She put her lunch tray down and sat opposite him.

'I hope you have everything you need,' she said, genuinely. 'If there's anything you want, please just ask me, and I'll do what I can. I expect we seem rather boring after all those glamorous film stars.'

'I don't get to meet many glamorous film stars I'm afraid. Well, I tell a lie – I did sit on the next table to Clive Brook one time, in a restaurant in Soho. He was actually -'

He didn't manage to finish his sentence, as the pilot of Q-Queenie interrupted, cutting in to ask the WAAF if she had a light for his cigarette. The girl immediately produced a lighter from her bag, and Jeremy noticed how the young pilot kept his eyes on her as the cigarette glowed into life, and they were both enveloped in a cloud of smoke. There was an awkward pause, as the pilot tried to assess whether he had interrupted anything, eyeing the young director carefully, before he thanked the girl, saying he'd see her again sometime, and pushed off to rejoin his crew at a nearby table.

'He looked like he wanted to spend a bit more time with you. Was I in the way?'

The girl looked up.

'I... no, please don't worry. He seems a nice enough boy, but...'

'But... not your type?'

She blushed. 'Oh no. It's just, well, a lot of nice boys come through the squadron. Doesn't always do to get to know them too well, if you understand what I mean.' There was a pause. 'Anyway...'

She smiled at him, and he detected a hurt beneath the smile, one which he got the feeling she didn't want to talk about.

Filming continued that afternoon in the crew room, getting shots showing Q-Queenie's crew in various states of relaxation, reading newspapers, playing cards, and sharing jokes. It was clear that Scotty Morgan, who was still calling the shots with Ziggy, was not interested in setting up fake scenes with dialogue. She seemed to be happy enough to capture a sense of atmosphere, of realistic action, shots that could run underneath a narration which would be written and voiced at a later point. Difficulties arose when some other crews found their way into the crew room barred for filming, and kicked up a fuss. They refused Scotty's offer to feature in the background, complaining that it was a poor show when their crew room was taken over by a bunch of idiots playing 'let's pretend'. The squadron leader's face darkened when he heard this, and he strode out after the recalcitrant airmen, and there was an awkward minute or so as everyone listened to him bawling them out in the corridor.

Jeremy noticed Scotty Morgan quietly tell Ziggy to turn the camera onto the faces of the Q-Queenie crew as they listened, exchanging nervous glances, and when the squadron leader returned, apologising for the unfortunate incident, there was a glint in her eye when she assured him that it had been no trouble at all; in fact, quite the opposite.

'That's all for today, thank you very much everybody. See you all bright and early in the morning – 8 o'clock on camera at the main gate for the arrival shots.'

Scotty Morgan offered Jeremy a roll-up from her tin. 'Well done, Jeremy, your first day in action. How d'you feel?'

He shrugged.

'That bad? We got through the day, didn't we?'

'Yes.'

'And we have material in the can?'

'Yes.'

68

'And nobody got killed.'

He looked at her.

'But you didn't get to do any of your fancy set ups?'

The young director looked around at the crew packing their equipment away. 'I didn't get to do anything really – you pretty much made sure of that.'

'Touchy.' Scotty Morgan blew a stream of smoke out of the side of her mouth. 'Well, ask yourself this. What did you learn today?'

'That I don't think I want to be a director anymore, not doing this kind of work anyway.'

'Fair enough,' said Scotty. 'That's up to you. So you didn't get to direct much. But you lived to fight another day. You're still here, I haven't fired you.'

He thought about this.

'We're gathering for a bit of a do in the Officer's Mess tonight, guests of the station commander, to celebrate a successful first day's shoot. 7.30 prompt, best bib and tucker. And cheer up Jeremy. It could have been worse.'

'What do you mean?'

'I could have let you carry on fannying around with your developing shot. And then where would we have been? See you in the mess.'

The young director had no intention of going to the mess for drinks that night. The day had been humiliating and depressing enough without having to pretend everything had been a success. But as he lay on his stiff, unyielding mattress, staring at the ceiling, his thoughts returned to those few moments he had shared with Hobson, the young WAAF. Amidst the chaos and gloom of the day her presence, and above all those eyes, that revealed sadness and hinted at the promise of other things at the same time, shone out like beacons of hope. At least she had seen something in him.

So it was with the vague hope that Hobson would be at the party that he smartened himself up and stepped out into the fresh evening air to head to the Officer's Mess. But when he arrived, even though the party was already under way, the young WAAF was nowhere to be seen, and he couldn't help feeling an overwhelming disappointment. Several members of the film crew, including Scotty Morgan, were in deep conversation with senior uniforms, although Jeanette, the continuity girl, he saw was sitting alone. He was on the point of leaving when she caught his eye and held up an empty glass. Unable to ignore her, he pushed through the crowd to order a couple of drinks at the bar, then joined her, quickly realising that they hadn't actually exchanged more than a couple of words until now. Indeed, he spent a good few minutes desperately trying to remember her name, before deciding that he didn't care anyway. He had often wondered why a woman who was clearly in her fifties should still be referred to as a 'girl', but wasn't sure this was the right moment to ask, and so as he listened to her story concerning her bombed-out mother coming to stay in her tiny Camden flat, he drank, his mind returning to the conversation he and Hobson had had in the canteen, and to the unusual and immediate understanding they'd seemed to share. Of all the people involved in this sad, sorry affair, she was the one he felt he could talk to, *wanted to talk to*. So when he looked up and the young WAAF was only a few yards away, standing at the squadron leader's side, his spirits immediately lifted.

'Hello. Someone's tail is wagging,' said the continuity girl. Jeremy shrugged the implication off, but the older woman continued. 'Pretty thing, I must say. Fancy your chances?'

But before the young director could reply, he saw Hobson turn with a smile to the pilot of Q-Queenie, who arrived with two glasses, one of which he gave to her, and immediately the two were heads bent together, laughing about something.

'Can't beat a man in a uniform, I suppose. Hard luck.' The continuity girl carried on with her tale of woe and the young director pretended to listen. He ordered more drinks from a passing waiter, which he proceeded to knock back rather too quickly, and couldn't help watching Hobson and the young pilot as they remained together. Although held in deep conversation with the pilot, the young WAAF, he thought, stole one or two quick glances in his direction, and at one point, he was sure, threw him a definite smile. He emptied his glass, and sank into the deep, comforting fug of self-pity.

'That's your cue,' said the continuity girl, and nudged him. The young WAAF was standing alone, looking at her glass, the pilot nowhere to be seen. 'Make your move before Biggles returns.'

'Hello,' said Hobson as he appeared next to her. 'Aren't you going to invite your friend to join us, she's all alone.'

Jeremy glanced back at Jeanette, who smiled and returned to her drink. 'Oh, well, I... I just wanted to say hello. And to say thank you for all your help today. We couldn't have done it without you.'

'Don't be silly, I only arranged the tea and biscuits with the NAAFI, hardly saved the day.' She laughed, and he noticed again how her face came alive at these moments.

'I'm not terribly good at these things,' he said. 'Do you think perhaps we might get some air?'

She nodded, and he took her arm, leading her through the crowd towards an outer door, and they stepped into the forgiving coolness of the evening.

'That was a good idea,' she said, 'I can breathe.' There was a pause, as they listened to the distant noise of the party.

'I'm afraid I don't know your name,' he said, eventually.

'Barbara,' she said.

'That's a lovely name,' he said.

'I hate it.' She grimaced. 'Makes one think of the Salvation Army.' She noted the look of incomprehension on his face. *Major Barbara*, the George Bernard Shaw play? I thought you would have known it.'

'Oh yes,' he remembered. 'They made a film of it recently, I believe. Wendy Hiller.'

'Yes, I saw it in town. The girls were winding me up for days afterwards, calling me Major,' she laughed, but he felt that she stopped herself too soon, as if she had been reminded of something, or someone else.

'I hope you don't mind me asking...'

She looked up. 'Try me.'

'At lunch, in the canteen, when that pilot asked you for a light and I said he seemed nice...' She looked at him. 'Well, I got the impression that there had perhaps been someone, in the past? You don't have to tell me if you don't want to.'

The young WAAF looked away, up into the night sky, and thought for a few moments. 'Yes, there was. I'd only just been posted here, and he was a pilot, rather good looking and of course he seemed to be... well, I was very fond of him. And then one night he didn't come back. His name was David.'

'I'm sorry. I shouldn't have asked,' he said, suddenly feeling very small. This girl, who was a good four or five years younger than him, seemed to be older in years and experience, to have lived so much more. He felt foolish, and wished he hadn't mentioned it, but if he was honest there was also a sense of jealousy in there. He wished, in a perverse way, that he could have been that dead pilot, who this beautiful girl had loved and obviously still did.

There was a pause, and they both became aware again of the sounds of the party inside. 'I'd expected that you would have been doing more of the actual directing today,' she said.

'You noticed,' he said.

'Hard not to,' she replied. 'I felt terribly for you, it must have been awfully embarrassing. You really haven't done anything like this before, have you?'

He looked away, unable to answer, and felt, not for the first time that day, that if he spoke, he might just burst into tears.

'Oh, I'm sorry, I didn't mean to upset you,' she said genuinely, and moved towards him, touching his arm. 'It'll all work out perfectly in the end, I'm sure you'll make a wonderful director. And one day I'll be watching a film and see your name on the screen, and I'll be able to say, I knew him when-'

She stopped as he kissed her, gently on the mouth. It was the briefest of kisses, as she pulled away quickly.

'I'm sorry,' he said, 'I shouldn't have done that.'

'That's alright,' she said. 'You obviously wanted to.' A moment later she moved to the door, saying she was out of cigarettes, and was gone.

After a few minutes, during which he cursed himself for being a stupid bloody fool, Jeremy went back into the mess, and saw that Hobson was once again with the young pilot of Q-Queenie, who was now joined by several other members of the crew. The young WAAF glanced over towards him and looked away again quickly.

'Hello boys,' said the young director, a little too loudly, and the crew all turned to look at him. 'Hope you're all enjoying yourselves. Good day's work by the way, you all did a terrific job.'

'If you can call it a job,' said the pilot. His strong Geordie accent only emphasised the disregard he had for the day's work and the contempt which he felt towards the young director. The other flyers laughed. Hobson put down her glass. 'Well, it's getting late, and I've got work to do tomorrow, so I think I'll call it a night.'

'Oh, don't go Barbara, not on my account anyway,' said the young director, and the WAAF noticed he was starting to slur his words. 'There was something I wanted to share, with you all actually, which I think is quite interesting in the light of what we are all doing.'

The airmen and the WAAF all looked at him, swaying ever so slightly on his feet.

'It's funny really, I hadn't seen it until now, but actually there is rather more that we – you flyers, and us film makers – have in common than you might think.'

'Really? And just what is that?'

'Well,' said the young director, warming to his theme, 'what have we been doing today?'

'Standing around like a bunch of lemons,' said the rear gunner, and the others laughed.

'No, no we weren't. We were *shooting*, which is after all what you air gunners do, when you're up there dealing with the night fighters and so on.' Sensing the flyers' reactions, the young WAAF tried to take him to one side. 'Perhaps you should call it a night, don't you think?'

'No, I haven't finished yet.' He raised his voice again. 'So, we work in shots, like you do, and our *ammunition*, if you like, our film stock, is kept in magazines, just as your bullets are. You see? But there's more. Before we start shooting, we go on a recce, short for reconnaissance obviously, which is exactly what you boys do before you fly out and bomb a target – the same again. But most obviously, the thing we have in common is we both work in crews – your bomber crew and our film crew – and it's exactly the same for us as it is for you – both crews are tight-knit teams where each man has to know his task down to the last detail, and everyone has to know that they can trust the others to get them safely through to the end of the job. Quite funny really, how similar we are, you and us, when you come to think about it.'

The party had fallen silent now, as one by one people began to sense a tension in the room. Scotty Morgan was staring at the young director with undisguised horror.

'Aye, and I'll tell you something that's really funny,' said the pilot, his voice suddenly loud in the unexpected silence. 'If your crew get something wrong, because someone forgets his lines or it starts to rain like, you can go for another take. Only when you're at twenty thousand feet in a Lancaster, with night fighters and the flak flying up at you, real shooting like, well if something goes wrong, we don't get a second chance. That's it. One take and it's a wrap, as you say.' He looked at the young WAAF, who was staring at the floor, face flushed. 'I'm sorry miss,' he said. 'Come on lads, I think we're done here.' He turned on his heel and the crew followed as one.

The young director looked around, aware now that the eyes of the room were upon him. A moment later Scotty Morgan was at his shoulder. 'Outside, now.' She strode off, pausing as she went to thank the station commander for a lovely evening.

'I'm sorry, Barbara,' the young director stammered. 'I don't know–'

'Just – don't say another word. It'll only make things worse.'

Jeremy made his way to the door, where he knew Scotty Morgan was waiting. A minute later the party had resumed and the embarrassing interlude involving the drunken director was forgotten.

At breakfast the next morning, a diligent observer would have noticed a slight change in the general atmosphere from previous days. Conversations were a little quieter, the usual laughter and banter a little more restrained; here and there airmen sat alone with their thoughts as they drank coffee or smoked.

Sitting in a group at their table the film crew were unaware of the almost imperceptible change in energy, until the squadron leader approached Scotty Morgan with the news that the crew of Q-Queenie would be unavailable until further notice. Orders had come from Group that the squadron was to be in readiness for operations and like the other crews, Q-Queenie's would be busy all day preparing for the raid.

'I see,' said Scotty Morgan. 'That's a bugger – for us, I mean. What do we do?'

'Well, you won't be able to leave the station, or make any phone calls,' said the squadron leader, 'Security, you know – I'd suggest you put your feet up and read a book?'

He was already on his way out when Scotty Morgan said, 'I say, what if-?'

'What if what?' the squadron leader stopped. Something had told him he knew what was coming.

'What if we followed them, the crew of Q-Queenie that is, as they do all the things they have to? It's exactly what we would be forced to fake otherwise.'

'You mean film the crew as they prepare for ops?'

'Why not? I imagine they'll be doing everything we'd want to include in our film – briefings, flying tests, final meal in the canteen and so on...'

The squadron leader stared at her as if she had lost her mind. 'Are you serious? We can't have a film crew getting in the way on a day like this, it's far too risky – sorry.'

'But you'd never even know we were there. We'd pare everything down to the essentials, no sound, no lights, just the camera, the operator and me. I promise we wouldn't get in the way.'

'But-'

'And you said yourself that we can't leave the station so I don't see how security would be compromised. If we get under your feet or are a problem in any way, I promise we will stop filming immediately.'

The squadron leader remembered the station commander telling him how she had come by the nickname 'Scotty'.

'I'll have to ask the station commander.'

'Thank you, I really do appreciate it.'

'But don't be surprised if he has a fit and throws you in the cells.'

Scotty Morgan smiled. 'I won't.'

The station commander gladly approved of Scotty Morgan's request, mainly on the grounds that if it meant one less day on his station it had to be a good thing; the squadron leader then had the unenviable job of informing the crew of Q-Queenie of the change of plan. As it happened, most of them had other things on their minds and couldn't care less about the film crew, apart from the pilot, who insisted on receiving a written assurance that the 'idiot with the beard' wouldn't be involved, before he would agree to the idea. The squadron leader duly scribbled out a chit, mentally noting that this pilot was turning out to be rather bloody minded and would have to be watched carefully.

Setting to immediately, and working alone, Scotty Morgan and Ziggy discreetly filmed the crew of Q-Queenie as they went about the business of preparing for their first operation. Tucking themselves in a corner here, or away to one side there, they set up the camera on a tripod or worked handheld, filming the crew as they attended briefings and discussions about the operation, collected parachutes and pulled on flying kit, shared a smoke and a joke after Q-Queenie's flying test. Always focusing on the crew, they were able to capture an accurate and entirely realistic record of what the boys were doing and feeling, without any sense of the enterprise being faked or dramatised. Scotty was delighted – this was exactly what she had wanted all along, and already she was mentally editing what she knew would be a decent short.

The young director, meanwhile, stared out of the window in his hut, catching occasional glimpses of the activity on the airfield and in the skies above, and going over in his mind how he could have made such a damned fool of himself last night. Was it jealousy, that Barbara seemed more interested in the young pilot and not him? Or petulance, a childish reaction to the way Scotty Morgan had humiliated him on set? Whatever, in saying what he'd said to the crew of Q-Queenie he had sealed his own fate. The dressing down he'd received from Scotty after the party, under the amused gaze of passing airmen, had been brutal and direct: his rude and selfish behaviour was unforgiveable, particularly given the conditions they were working under, and they'd be lucky if the RAF didn't withdraw their co-operation altogether and the film would have to be abandoned. She was hugely disappointed in him and saw no reason why he shouldn't be sent back to London on the first available train. He had begged her to reconsider, but she was implacable. He was off the picture, and she was taking over as director.

He had had his chance, in more ways than one, and blown it.

In the early evening, around five o'clock, the crews were driven to dispersal and hung around until they got the order to start up. Scotty and Ziggy filmed the crew of Q-Queenie as they chatted and played cards, and kept shooting as they climbed aboard, the ground crew cleared the pilot to start up the engines and the Lancaster pulled into the queue for take-off, finally climbing into the darkening sky.

'I've cut there,' said Ziggy, quietly, exhausted and feeling the strain of staring through an eyepiece all day.

'Check the gate?' said Scotty Morgan.

'Why bother?' said the Czech. 'We can't go again, to coin a phrase.' He smiled.

Scotty Morgan eased her shoulders. 'Don't remind me. Well, these boys won't be back for at least seven hours, and I hear a drink or three calling.'

When they entered the Officer's Mess they found the young director sitting alone with a tonic water.

'I thought I'd confined you to barracks,' said Scotty Morgan. 'You did,' said the young director. 'I just... well, I've been thinking, and I wanted to have a word with you.'

'I don't want to hear any more apologies, Jeremy, it's too late for that.'

'No, I understand that. I was wondering, how did today go?'

'Wonderful, thank you. Ziggy and I have got some great stuff in the can. We followed the crew around and just shot them doing what they did.'

'So I heard,' said the young director.

'A new bomber crew's first operation, exactly as it happened. No interference, just raw actuality, what you see is what you get. Ziggy's a genius – he got some terrific unguarded moments, didn't you Zig?'

The Czech nodded, sprawling back in his armchair, eyes closed.

'We left the boys as they flew east, headed for the Rhur, and we're pretty sure we've enough stock left to see the Lancaster's return and catch the moments as the crew set their boots on solid ground again. Fade to black, closing titles, go home.'

'Well, that's what I wanted to talk to you about,' said the young director. 'If you don't mind.'

'Go on.'

'It seems to me you've got a great little film, but you're just missing one beat, perhaps the most important part of the story.'

Scotty Morgan stared at him. 'And what is that?'

He raised his eyebrows, and smiled, as if stating the obvious: 'The operation itself.'

'Forget it,' said Ziggy, 'Can you imagine the hoops we'd have to go through to film a crew on a bombing raid? It'd never happen.' Scotty Morgan said nothing, her stare remaining fixed on the young director.

'But that's just it,' he said. 'Don't you see? I've been thinking, and my idea is that we film the raid from the crew's point of view, in the cockpit, but we don't actually fly over Germany, we recreate the experience on the ground.'

Silence.

'We set up Q-Queenie in a hangar, and cover the cockpit with blackout cloth – they must have tons of the stuff on the station – so it looks like night. Ziggy can set up lights to recreate searchlights and flak bursts and so on, and we shoot the crew at their posts, doing what they do, as you say, as if they were on a real raid.'

He sat back, waiting for a response. When none was forthcoming, he continued, 'I also thought that maybe we could film Hobson, the WAAF, waiting nervously for the crew to return. She's awfully photogenic, don't you think Ziggy? And she knows better than anybody the emotion we'd be after.'

Scotty Morgan opened her tobacco tin, selected a roll-up and struck a match, taking a deep drag and blowing a cloud of smoke into the air.

'Very good Jeremy. But you really don't get it, do you?'

'I thought that was what you were after, for me to show how I could be spontaneous, and improvise in the face of obstacles.'

'This film is about the crew, and all the other crews, not just in this squadron, but on airfields across the country, who are fighting this bloody war. Not about Jeremy, a first-time director whom nobody has heard nor cares about.'

'That's not fair,' said the young director, his cheeks burning.

'Life's not fair,' Scotty Morgan replied. 'Those boys in Q-Queenie will tell you that, if they come back. But your ego has been hurt and you can't see beyond that, and until you do I doubt you'll ever be a good director.'

She looked at him, crumpled, his eyes filling with tears.

'Oh, don't get me wrong, you'll probably work, in advertising or features, and you'll make oodles of money and be a success. But you'll never be good. Ever. So if you don't mind...'

And with that she turned back to her camera operator.

The young director left the mess, and after wandering around the airfield was eventually challenged by an armed service policeman, who told him in no uncertain terms to return to his quarters. He did as he was told, packing ready for the early train to London, before spending the rest of the sleepless night staring at the shadows on the ceiling.

Scotty Morgan and Ziggy were soon joined by the rest of the film crew, where they happily drank and told stories about nightmare shoots and people they'd never want to work with again, but strangely no-one bothered to mention the young director. Shortly before midnight Scotty put her head down for a couple of hours' sleep, setting the alarm to wake her in good time to join Ziggy at the dispersal for the return of Q-Queenie.

In the Watch Office at around 2am, Corporal Hobson placed a mug of hot chocolate on the station commander's desk and took her seat next to the squadron leader.

'Still no word from C for Charlie, sir?'

'No, that makes two we've not heard from.'

Meanwhile, nearly four hundred miles away, in the black skies a thousand feet over northern Holland, the wireless operator on Q-Queenie lay sprawled across his desk, as dead as his smashed wireless set. A few feet away, Sergeant William Keene, the pilot, tried not to think about the decapitated body of his flight engineer lying next to him, and thought instead of a girl in Gateshead, as he wrestled with the controls, trying desperately to keep the dying Lancaster's nose up.

Ubendum Wemendum

'You was talking in your sleep again last night, Arthur.'

Arthur Elliot looked up. His big, oily fingers held an enamel mug of steaming tea close to his lips. 'Really?'

'Sign of a guilty conscience, if you ask me,' said the fitter, whose name was Walter, but was known to everyone as Shag.

'What do you mean?'

'You heard.'

'You're talking bollocks,' Arthur said, taking a sip of the scalding tea.

'You're the one was talking bollocks,' said Shag, grinning. 'Never heard such a load of nonsense.'

'I wasn't making any sense then?' Arthur said. If Shag hadn't been concentrating on his bully beef sandwich he might have detected a note of anxiety in his mate's question.

'Even less than you do when you're awake,' Shag replied, 'if that's possible.' He swallowed down a mouthful of sandwich and looked at his mate. 'Everything alright, Arthur?'

'Fine, thanks.'

'Just you're a bit quiet these days.'

'I said I'm fine.' Arthur glanced at his watch. 'We better get going.'

Arthur and the rest of the ground crew emptied the dregs of their mugs onto the grass, each incanting the words 'God bless Jimmy,' as they did so. If asked, none of the men could quite explain what this meant, but like most superstitions they knew it brought good luck if they said it, or more importantly, it might bring bad luck if they didn't.

They returned the empty mugs to Ruby in the NAAFI wagon and turned back towards the Lancaster sitting at dispersal. The rain, which had started not long after they began work that morning, was set in for the day now, and a cold, biting wind whipped the icy drops across the wide, flat airfield, stinging wherever it caught exposed skin on faces or hands. The Lancaster had a snag list as long as Arthur's arm, the result of a bad night over Dortmund from which two other machines failed to return. Despite the weather, the mechanics worked quickly but efficiently, each knowing that if they didn't do their job to the best of their capabilities, they might not see their aircraft, and by implication, the men who flew it, return from the next op. The work was carried out to the constant soundtrack of chatter, whistling and drilling, punctuated by the odd shout and loud metallic crash as a tool was thrown into its box, and at dispersal points spread out around the windswept airfield more ground crews were doing similar work on other bombers.

True, he'd have preferred to be working in the comparative comfort of a hangar, but Arthur felt at home here, had done ever since his posting to the aerodrome in the middle of '41. Engines, oil and spanners were all he ever seemed to have known, or had time for, or loved. Leaving school in Southend at 15 he knew he was going to be a mechanic, like his dad, and was soon apprenticed to a firm of engineers, working on trucks and cars by day and renovating a broken-down motorbike in his dad's shed at night. Arthur senior had presented him with the sorry-looking 350cc BSA on his birthday, and the two of them spent hour upon hour tinkering away at the beast, scrounging a part here and improvising a repair there. They would work long into the evening, while his mother brought them mugs of tea and cheese sandwiches, unable to quite understand their fascination for the dirty lump of metal but glad of the peace and quiet it afforded her. For their part, working on the bike allowed them to be together; focused on the all-important job of fixing the machine, often going for long intervals without exchanging a single word, they always ended each session in the assured knowledge that they had done a good job.

Although he now wore a blue uniform under his overalls and had a forage cap perched on the back of his head, he was essentially living the same life, except the engines he worked on today were massive Merlins, and the tea and sandwiches were supplied by the NAAFI. Life in the spanner brigade was hard but it suited him. His permanently oil-stained fingers were used to digging into the sharp unforgiving recesses of an engine, and months of working in all weathers (but mostly cold and wet, it seemed) had inured him to all but the most extreme pain and suffering. Of course, he knew how to grumble and complain like the best of them, but even when the cold was getting too much for him, the satisfaction he got from seeing the Lanc he had spent hours slaving over, lift into the sky on its great black wings, more than made up for the agony of bleeding fingers. That, and a mug of hot tea, a smoke, and a laugh with the lads, that is.

Until recently.

Arthur had a reputation amongst the other erks as a cheerful type, always ready with a smile and a joke no matter what the circumstances. He wasn't particularly outgoing, preferring his own company to that of the crowd, and it had been said of him that 'you don't get to know Arthur, he gets to know you,' but he was popular and well-known around the station. From time to time an introspective, slightly melancholy element in his character would reveal itself, and he'd decline the lads' invitation to join them on a jaunt into town, preferring to be on his own, but usually it was 'good old Arthur.' Recently though, the darker side of his personality had come to dominate, and Arthur spent more time in his own company.

'A good woman, that's what you need Arthur,' Shag would say. 'She'll soon sort you out. I'll have a word with Joyce in stores and see if we can set you up with one of her pals.'

There had been someone, not long after he'd joined the squadron; a Welsh girl called Beryl, who drove a tractor delivering the trains of bomb trolleys from the bomb dump to the Lancs at dispersal. Beryl, it turned out, as well as having a winning smile and lovely green eyes, was something of a talker, and almost without knowing how it had happened, Arthur found they were going to the pictures, and then again, and Beryl joked that 'people would start to talk.' Although they went into town regularly, they preferred walking together in the fields and woods around the station. Arthur discovered that as well as being a talker Beryl was also a good listener, and on their long walks he soon found himself, at her encouragement, discussing things he had never talked about before. Things like what he thought about, and felt; not just the war, but more personal things, about himself.

Having grown up on a small dairy farm, Beryl was well-versed in the countryside, and knew all the names of the trees and flowers, which fascinated Arthur. Although he could tell an oak from a pine, and a daisy from a dandelion, that was pretty much as far as his knowledge went, and Beryl laughed in a way that made Arthur ache as she tested him. For his part, Arthur had an almost encyclopaedic knowledge of birds, many of which he could identify by their appearance and calls, as well as by their eggs, the result of a youth spent roaming the hedges and streams near his home, armed with a small book on British birds which had been presented by his Sunday school. He still had the book, which was one of the few personal possessions he had brought with him when he joined the RAF, packed into a pannier on his BSA. He didn't quite know why, but he enjoyed flicking through the pages, and showing the simple but evocative illustrations of the birds and their eggs to Beryl on their long, lazy walks. One gentle, sunny afternoon in May, when they were sitting in the shade of an ancient barn, Beryl had noticed that in between the kisses, Arthur's attention wasn't focused entirely on her. Worried that perhaps there was something he wasn't telling her, she asked him what was on his mind, and he willingly confessed. He had been watching a tiny brown bird which kept returning to the same spot in a nearby hedge, and knowing what this meant, he got up, telling her to follow him. Pushing through the white froth of May blossom, he reached deep into the branches and vicious spikes of the hawthorn and managed to slip his fingers into the tiny cup of a wren's nest, retrieving a single miniature white and reddish-brown speckled egg. Silently, as if holding something sacred, he slipped the warm jewel into her hand.

'It's beautiful,' she said, turning it around in the cup of her hand with her finger. 'Can you believe anything so small could have a baby bird inside it?'

'It's yours,' he said. 'I'll blow it, and you can keep it forever, to remember today.'

But her smile dropped as she told him that it was bad luck to take an egg, even one, and so, like a naughty boy, he pushed back into the hedge to replace the egg before it went cold. *Except he hadn't actually put it back.* Something made him keep it, concealing the egg in his big mechanic's hands and then hiding it in the safety of his handkerchief when Beryl wasn't looking. Back in the Nissen hut that evening, where he and the other erks slept, he had carefully pricked a tiny hole in each end of the egg with a needle and blown the contents out onto a page of newspaper. A small stain of blood lay in the mess of yolk and albumen, which he screwed up and threw into the stove. He stuffed some kapok in an empty matchbox, laid the egg in it, and placed it on the shelf above his bed. He thought it would be nice to open it from time to time and remember the best day that he and Beryl had yet spent together.

Arthur and Beryl saw a lot more of each other, and he felt that things might become serious between them. A few weeks later they even spent a weekend back at her family farm near Camarthen, driving across country on his motorbike, with Beryl desperately clinging onto Arthur for dear life all the way. The farm, just a couple of dark slate buildings and a few fields of cows nestling in a tiny valley, seemed like paradise to Arthur, and as they leaned on the gate she spoke for the first time about how much the farm meant to her, and that one day, after the war, she'd come back to live here and raise a family. But she didn't lace her fingers in between his as she did when they walked near the airfield, and although he couldn't quite say why, he felt something of a distance growing between them.

He had not felt comfortable with her parents either, who seemed to view him with barely disguised suspicion. On the Saturday night, while he was out in the yard having a smoke, he thought he heard raised words between Beryl and her mother, although all seemed smiles when he stepped back into the parlour. But he and Beryl had their first real argument when she refused to risk her life again on 'that bloody bike', and insisted on getting the train back, leaving Arthur to explain to the lads why he had returned from his romantic weekend alone. 'Bad luck, Arthur,' said Shag, 'I thought you and that Welsh rarebit were good together.' Although they kissed and made up when Beryl returned the next day, Arthur couldn't help feeling that somehow things had changed between them, and not for the better.

And then a few days later, as Beryl was unhooking a bomb-trolley from her tractor, something slipped, there was a crash of cold, hard metal and she lost two fingers from her right hand. The accident had happened some distance away from Arthur's Lancaster, P-Popsie, and when he heard he had run to the sick bay, where he found Beryl with a bandaged hand, dosed to the eyeballs with morphine, surrounded by her WAAF friends. For some undefinable reason Arthur had felt responsible for the accident, even though Beryl insisted she had been a fool for not wearing her gloves. The WAAF girls put that down to bad luck, Beryl usually being so diligent about safety. But Arthur still felt guilty, and it hit him all the harder when a few days later he heard that Beryl was leaving the WAAF and had returned to Wales without saying goodbye. 'Bad luck, Arthur,' the lads said, when they heard. A letter from Beryl, apologising for not saying goodbye lifted his spirits somewhat, and they continued to write to each other for a few weeks, but reading between the lines he got the clear sense that her family blamed the war, and by implication, it seemed, himself for the dreadful injuries their girl had suffered. When he offered to ride over to Camarthen and see her on his next leave she quickly kiboshed the idea, and it soon became clear that the flame that had kept the relationship alive had guttered and died; Beryl's letters became shorter and more infrequent, until they stopped altogether. It was now six months since he had last heard from her.

He could do with having Beryl to talk to now, he reflected. Somehow he had never felt embarrassed when she encouraged him to talk about his feelings, and he needed to talk right now. Although his mates had noticed lately that there was something preoccupying Arthur, they hadn't felt it was their place to ask him what was wrong, or like Shag, had simply assumed Arthur's problem was that 'he wasn't getting any.'

The change had come over Arthur not long after the accident in which P-Popsie had been lost, crashing shortly after take-off on a Night Flying Test. The accident had hit the ground crew hard, coming as it did out of the blue like that. Somehow it was easier to accept the loss of an aircraft when you'd been stood waiting on a lonely airfield in the early hours, half-expecting the inevitable confirmation that the aircraft wouldn't return. To lose P-Popsie in this unexpected way, so close to home, and to be part of the operation that had to retrieve the bodies and clear away the wreckage, made the loss all the harder to bear. But the ground crew had got on with it; there had been a few days during which they shared stories about the old crate's foibles and peculiarities, and talked about how they'd miss her. They also remembered the crew, a little less fondly it had to be said, and even hazarded possible explanations for the crash.

It was during one of these conversations, sitting around the pot-bellied stove in their Nissen hut, that Arthur had suddenly felt his blood turn cold.

'There was nothing wrong with P-Popsie,' said one of the lads. 'Everyone said so - there was no explanation for the crash.'

'Gremlins.'

'Nah. Don't believe in 'em,' said Shag.

'No-one's blaming us though,' said another.

'We all did our job,' said a third.

'These things happen, especially in war. You can't explain it,' said Shag.

'Bloody bad luck.'

'That's it.'

'Yeah, bleedin' bad luck.'

The lads had decided to go into town that night and drown their sorrows at the Ram, but Arthur had said he didn't feel like it, and despite the lads' attempts to change his mind, he was insistent, and spent the evening alone, lying on his bed. He couldn't get the image of that new air gunner out of his mind – the lad from up north who had given him the letter. He'd thought nothing of it at the time, and had just placed the letter on the gunner's bed when he heard the explosion, followed by the wail of sirens. But now he couldn't get the lad's face out of his head, looking up with that innocent smile, full of excitement before his first flight on P-Popsie.

Bloody bad luck...

He reached up to the shelf above his head and took down the matchbox, sliding it open to reveal the tiny, precious wren's egg sitting safely in its nest of wadding.

'It's bad luck to take an egg, even one,' Beryl had said, and he could still remember the look of horror on her face when he had even suggested such a thing. If only he had put the egg safely back into the nest, as she had wanted him to, everything that had followed could have been avoided. So what did his action that afternoon, and the subsequent deception, say about himself? That he was not the good bloke that everyone seemed to see; he was a liar, and untrustworthy. He had deceived Beryl, the only truly good thing in his life and someone he told himself he loved – how could he do that to her? His actions, and the bad luck that followed had caused the dreadful accident that resulted in her leaving the station and ended their courtship. He stared at the egg, thinking about what the lads had said, and with every twist and turn

that his mind took he felt sicker and more desperate. Was he bad luck? Everything seemed to add up to it – the sudden change in Beryl's feelings for him, and her terrible accident. The lads had noticed that themselves. It was all bad luck, perhaps even…

He took the egg out of the matchbox, and held it carefully in his big, gnarled mechanic's fingers. Holding it up to the bare lightbulb he could see through the thin shell, seeing that it was empty, as empty as he felt deep inside now. He had taken it, he had told himself, as something to remind him of the lovely, beautiful, pure thing that he and Beryl had. And it had done exactly the opposite. He could see nothing except misery and failure and the awful emptiness deep in his soul, the emptiness of a hollow man who deserved nothing, least of all the love of a good woman or the friendship of his mates.

But that was only the half of it. The truth was his bad luck had caused P-Popsie to crash that day, to fall out of the sky and kill seven men in a huge explosion. He felt sick as he imagined the last few seconds each of those men had known, as their machine plummeted towards the ground, and they knew they were going to die and there was nothing they could do about it. What were they thinking? Did they even have time for a last prayer, or to think of their loved ones, wives, girlfriends, parents, children? They probably only knew what he was feeling now – a dreadful sickening fear.

And yet he deserved what he was suffering. How could he continue to pretend to be innocent when he knew that the blood of those men was on his unlucky hands? He wasn't worthy to look any of his mates in the eye again, let alone the crew who would soon arrive to fly the replacement P-Popsie.

If people knew what he had done, what it meant… but they couldn't know. If he told any of the lads about this they would only laugh, thinking he was off his head. Or worse, they would say that he wasn't a man to be trusted, a man unworthy of being part of the team. He would forever be bad luck, shunned, isolated, sent to Coventry and made to suffer in miserable solitude until he was posted away from the station, if another squadron would have him.

Slowly, as the tears filled his eyes, he crushed the egg in his fingers, until all that remained were tiny fragments of shell.

Arthur lay on the bed all evening, staring at the roof of the hut, dreadful thoughts and images flying around inside his head until eventually he fell into an exhausted sleep. For a few precious hours he forgot his troubles as sleep did its job of allowing his brain to rest. The following morning though, within seconds of waking, the reality of his situation hit him like a wave. *He had caused P-Popsie to crash*. With stark clarity, all his fears returned to haunt his day, magnified and made all the more painful as his mates, unpreoccupied by any mental torments of their own, got on with their day.

He strove desperately to find ways to take his mind off these dark, obsessive thoughts. He found that when he was working, he could concentrate and focus on the practical job in hand for a few precious minutes; there would be moments when the cold memory of his guilt would come at him from out of nowhere, but someone would say something or crack a joke and he could soon lose himself in his work again, and so he looked forward more than ever to a busy day with a long list of snags to fix. He also found that he preferred days when the weather was particularly bad and made working harder, as it gave him something to fight against.

The replacement crew for P-Popsie arrived, and Arthur found that he hung back when the usual introductions were made, avoiding eye contact and not bothering to remember their names. The crew thought him a bit odd, but thought nothing more of his behaviour, preferring to concentrate on the business of flying P-Popsie.

The times when he was not working were the worst – at breakfast, in the canteen, or during tea or lunch breaks. In the evenings he now gladly accepted the lads' offer of a trip to the Ram, indeed was often the first to suggest it, and he threw himself a little too energetically into the drinking, the darts and the banter. And then he would be back in the hut, lying in his bed, trying to will the comforting blanket of sleep to descend over him. Watching the regular station football matches provided him with an outlet for the emotional conflict that was screwing his insides up: he would yell and curse from the side lines, losing himself in the game in a way which his mates hadn't seen before. And he took to long rides on his motorbike, speeding dangerously around the roads and lanes that he and Beryl had once walked along. The physical thrill of speed, and the danger of never quite knowing if anything was around the corner took his mind off his worries, but once back on the station it wasn't long before they crept back.

Sometimes as he rode, he thought about how easy it would be to end it all; just a simple flick of the handlebars and it would all be over. Lights out, curtains... And once, out at the dispersal point, as the Lancaster started up its engines, he found himself watching the mighty propellors cutting through the air. If he stepped forward now, into the path of those blades...

At other times a less extreme solution to his suffering would present itself: he should simply confess his guilt to a mate, or report sick to the MO, or even walk into the Guard Room and hand himself over to the warrant sergeant. If nothing else, the simple act of admitting his secret would bring relief; whatever punishments the authorities could inflict would never be as severe as the misery of his mental torment. Perhaps, he told himself, his confession would simply be met with derision and a shaking of the head, as people would think that he had lost it. 'Confessing to being "bad luck"? Arthur Elliot belongs in the funny farm.' But he had heard stories about what they did to folk who'd lost it – they'd be put in a straightjacket, locked up in a padded cell, sedated with drugs. He'd even heard that in some cases they attached electrical wires to your head and shocked the demons out of you, until eventually there was nothing left but a shell, as empty and lifeless as that damned wren's egg.

So when Shag had dropped the bombshell about talking

in his sleep, Arthur entered a new chamber of hell. What if, in his nocturnal ramblings, he said something that revealed his guilt? What if he actually spoke out loud the words that he had until now kept firmly inside his head, *saying that he was responsible for the crash of P-Popsie*. 'A sign of a guilty conscience,' Shag had said, that was why people talked in their sleep. Arthur spent the rest of the day worrying about this. The brain had a way of letting uncomfortable thoughts to the surface, that was what a lot of his dreams and nightmares were about, he was sure. So if his brain could make him dream about things he was obsessed with, wasn't it equally possible that it could make him talk about them in his sleep?

Maybe it would be possible to stop himself from talking in his sleep? If he thought hard, and told himself not to do it, would that work? No, he decided, it was logical that the more he tried *not* to talk about something in his sleep, that would be exactly what he *would* talk about. There was no way around it. At some point, it seemed obvious, he was going to confess his terrible secret while he was asleep, and there was nothing he could do about it.

He watched Shag while he was working. He was a happy bloke, a man of simple pleasures (most of which revolved around women). Perhaps, if he did hear Arthur say something about the crash, he would assume it was just more nonsense. But if he heard the same thing repeatedly, night after night? Surely Shag would work out that there was some significance to these apparently nonsensical ramblings? What would he do? Would he tell Arthur, or keep it to himself? Or would he tell someone else, one of the other lads, or the MO perhaps? That could only lead to the Guard Room or the padded cell, and once again Arthur's stomach turned over as he was caught in the vicious circle of his obsessive thoughts.

The solution, when it presented itself to Arthur, was surprisingly simple. *He wouldn't sleep*.

For the next week, when the lads turned in, Arthur pretended to go to sleep. He waited until the snores told him they were all off, and then lay as long as he could, eyes open, staring into the blackness. When tiredness was starting to close his eyes, he got a book and read it by dim torchlight, under the blanket. When that failed, he would start to write, scribbling letters to his family in Southend, something he hadn't done since things ended with Beryl. Once he was caught, when one of the lads got up for the ablutions and saw the torchlight before Arthur could switch it off, but nothing was said, and the adrenalin rush kept him awake for the rest of the night.

Sometimes, when the waves of tiredness were especially hard to hold back, he would get up and wander outside the hut, and on quiet nights he would stand and listen to the sounds of the country. He got to recognise the calling of tawny owls, one to another, from the woods at the edge of the airfield, and the unnerving screeching of foxes. Sometimes, far in the distance, so far he couldn't quite tell the direction the sound was coming from, he heard the unmistakable drone of Merlin engines. At this hour it could only be a Lancaster from another airfield, returning from an op. Once or twice he detected something 'off' on the engine note, or a worrying drop out, and he knew that the Lancaster was in trouble, and he said a silent prayer that they'd make it home.

In the morning, as the others woke and readied themselves for work, he would feel relieved, sure in the knowledge that his secret was safe for another day. Of course, sleepless nights meant tired days – he found himself yawning uncontrollably by mid-morning, and he could be miles away when someone asked him a question. Worse though, he became forgetful, and small mistakes crept into his work – Chiefy would have to tell him to have another go, or even to start a job all over again, which was most unlike Arthur.

He took to wandering off on his own at lunchbreak, looking for somewhere quiet for an hour's kip, but he often felt worse when he woke up, and sometimes he was caught napping on the job. Once Shag found him curled up and spark out in the tail of the Lancaster, and Arthur had to get him to swear that he wouldn't tell Chiefy. Shag promised he wouldn't say anything, but warned Arthur that he couldn't go on like this, whatever the problem was. Later that day Arthur froze when the warrant sergeant and a couple of service policemen pulled up at the dispersal point in a lorry. A few words were exchanged with Chiefy, and Arthur felt a jolt go through his body as the sergeant glanced in his direction. He was ready to give himself up when the warrant sergeant called up to the man working alongside Arthur, an electrician named Shaw, telling him *to get himself down here sharpish!* The erk cursed under his breath, before downing tools and sliding down the wing and into the open arms of the service policemen. The warrant sergeant informed Shaw he was on a charge, having been absent without leave; the lads all knew he'd had to go back to Birkenhead at the weekend to sort out a bloke who was seeing his wife, but hadn't expected he'd be hauled up for it. Watching Shaw being driven off in the lorry, Arthur couldn't help wishing it had been him on his way to the Guard Room.

Shortly afterwards, the crew of P-Popsie arrived and took possession of the aircraft for a routine air test. Ladders, bicycles, tools and equipment were cleared out of the Lancaster's path as the crew climbed aboard and took their stations. Arthur stood watching, as if in a trance, as one by one the engines were started up. The enormous propellor blades first stuttered, then windmilled, before with a burst of flame and a cloud of blue smoke from the exhausts, they snarled into ferocious life. The pilot signalled for the chocks to be pulled away and increased the revs, and the deafening roar of the Merlins drowned out all other sound. Staring at the almost invisible blur of whirling steel, Arthur felt that everything in his life was being focused down to this moment. The smiling face of the young air gunner, the burning wreckage of P-Popsie lying in the blackened corn stubble, the look in Beryl's eyes when he offered her the egg, all these things started to fade and retreat from his mind as the deadly spinning disc of metal swung round and drew nearer...

The next thing Arthur knew, he was lying on the

ground, with Shag holding him down, staring at him, his mouth moving soundlessly. Shag looked angry and seemed to be swearing at Arthur, but he couldn't make out any words over the tremendous noise of the Merlins. Above Arthur the mighty black wing of the Lancaster moved slowly, throwing him into shadow before blinding him as the sun reappeared, and then Shag was pulling him to his feet and dragging him away towards a fuel bowser. He sat Arthur down on the running board and waited until the Lancaster had moved sufficiently far enough away from them to speak.

'That was very bloody nearly an 'orrible mess,' said Shag, 'Good luck I was there to see you. What were you thinking?'

Arthur didn't say anything. In a strange way he felt he had been robbed of something. There was nothing he could say that could possibly explain that and not sound insane.

'Arthur? What the hell's wrong? You know better than to get in the way of those props. Didn't you see me waving?'

'He's been like a zombie all day,' said another fitter, standing close by. 'That was a close shave.'

'Do us a favour and find a flask of tea,' said Shag, keen not to have an audience. 'Arthur looks like he could do with it.'

The man wandered off and Shag sat down next to Arthur, who stared ahead, into the middle distance, as Shag had seen him doing so often in recent days. 'Bloody hell Arthur,' he said, 'What were you playing at?'

Eventually Arthur spoke, quietly. 'You should have let me die. It would have made everything better.'

'Better?' said Shag.

'For me, you, everyone. The world. I'm bad luck.'

Shag considered this. 'Is this about that Welsh rarebit? I thought you'd be over her by now.'

Arthur smiled, still staring ahead. 'Forget it, Shag. You don't understand.'

'Try me,' said Shag. 'What's happened?'

Arthur heard the words Shag was saying, and deep

down in him there was an urge to speak, to say what had happened to him, but he just couldn't start. It was all too terrifying, more terrifying than the prospect of instant oblivion which the deadly propellor blades had offered. The words that had been whirling and echoing around in his head for all this time, but which he had been repressing for fear they would be heard, just wouldn't come now. His brain was trying to send a message to his mouth, but still the words would not come out. He felt that if he said anything the world would come crashing down on his head.

The other fitter returned with a mug of tea. 'I put three sugars in it,' he said, placing the mug in Arthur's hands. 'He don't look good.'

'Cheers mate,' said Shag. 'Give us a sec, would you?'

The fitter moved off, and Shag watched as Arthur automatically raised the mug to his lips and took a sip of tea.

'Take your time.'

Arthur swallowed the hot, sweet liquid, and as it warmed his chest and stomach, there came a memory of an evening in his dad's workshed, before the war, as they drank tea and ate sandwiches during a break from working on the bike. There had been something on young Arthur's mind, something he felt too embarrassed to talk to his pals about, and as he and his dad seemed to be getting so much closer these days, fixing the bike, he had finally summoned up the courage to broach the difficult subject. Without introduction, he stammered out the question, staring at the bike, aware that his cheeks were burning, and when he finally looked at his father, was shocked to see that the man's face was white, and he seemed unable to speak. Eventually his dad got up, walked to the shed door and turned to his son. 'Don't ever speak to me like that again,' he said. 'Ever.' And he walked back into the house, leaving young Arthur trembling, confused and feeling more guilty than before.

'That tea working?' said Shag.

Finally Arthur spoke. 'I haven't been sleeping.'

'I can see that. You've been wandering around in a daze

all week. You should see the MO, he can give you some tablets.'

'It's not that I *can't* sleep. I've been stopping myself.'

'Stopping yourself from sleeping?'

'Yes.'

'But why?'

Arthur paused. He felt like he was standing on the edge of a precipice. 'Because...'

'Go on.'

'Because I'm afraid of what I might say in my sleep.' There was a pause as he felt Shag scrutinising him, confused. 'That sounds silly, doesn't it, but I'm serious.'

'Dunno,' said Shag. 'First time I ever heard of anything like that. What are you afraid of saying?'

Arthur turned to look at his friend, for the first time, and Shag saw fear in his eyes.

'I won't tell anyone', he said. 'Promise. You can trust me.'

Arthur took the next step, raising his foot over the precipice. 'I'm bad luck.'

'Right...' said Shag. 'And how d'you make that out?'

Over the next few minutes, sitting on the running board of the fuel bowser as the activity of the airfield went on around them, Arthur told his friend everything. He started slowly, struggling at first to find the words to explain about the egg, and how stupid he had felt when Beryl rejected it, and that that was where the bad luck started; about the disastrous weekend in Wales and then Beryl's accident and the end of their relationship. Soon the words were coming more easily as he talked about how he'd really liked that girl, and had blown it, stupidly, because deep down he was a bad person and couldn't be trusted, and he had brought bad luck on them. And when he talked about P-Popsie, and his overwhelming sense of guilt that he had brought its crew bad luck, that *he* had caused the Lancaster to fall out of the sky for no reason, and that it was his fault those seven lads had copped it, the words came out in a torrent, accompanied by tears. He cried as he described how he couldn't get the idea out of his head, and how he had been haunted by the guilty image of that new air gunner, smiling up at him, and that he thought he would never be able to forget it, at least until he saw those propellor blades...

By the end of the story the tears were running freely down Arthur's cheeks. He wiped them away with the sleeve of his overalls, but they continued to come. He looked up at Shag for the first time since his confession, expecting him to laugh, or to get up and head off to the Guard Room or the Sick Bay. But Shag just sat there, thinking about what he had heard.

'You going to say something?' sniffed Arthur.

'*Ubendum Wemendum*,' said Shag, eventually.

'Eh?'

'You know, the Ground Crew's motto. You bend 'em, we mend 'em. We work all the hours God sends, in all weathers, keeping those bleedin' machines flying. And we tell the aircrew, you bring 'em back in one piece, or there'll be hell to pay. And sometimes they do and sometimes they don't, and we have to live with that. Yeah, we pretend we don't care about those flying types, we don't trust 'em with our aeroplanes, but we know that ain't true. So one night a crew doesn't come back, and the Adjutant writes a bunch of letters to the families and the loved ones... your son was a fine chap, and he'll be missed by everyone in the squadron, blah blah blah. Fair enough, they need comfort in their hour of grief, to make sense of their loss. But what about us, eh? Who says to us, really sorry about your loss lads, you must be gutted you'll never see that crew again. And do we sit around and have a cry about it..? Do we hell.'

Arthur thought again about the air gunner. He couldn't say he knew him, the lad was new to the crew, and it was his first flight on P-Popsie. But he'd asked him to take care of his letter, and although it was only a small thing, he'd felt there'd been a connection between them. What Shag was saying made sense, sort of.

'No, Arthur, we just slag 'em off for not bringing our plane back and getting themselves killed, then get on with the replacement and tell the new crew they'll have to do better than the last lot and not lose this kite. And so it goes on, round and round. It's madness, don't you see, Arthur? Bloody madness, and you can't make sense of it. Yeah, something went wrong with P-Popsie. Mechanical failure perhaps, a part gets to the end of its life and bang! Or human error, by the pilot or maybe even, God forbid, by one of us – but what good does it do to blame someone? These things happen, get on with it. They might get shot down by a bleedin' night fighter, catch some flak over the target. That your fault? Course not. Yeah, it's bad luck. But bad luck is just that – it's when bad stuff happens for no reason. Nothing to do with Arthur Elliot or a bleedin' bird's egg for Christ's sake.'

Arthur smiled. 'You reckon?'

'Course I do. How do you think I get through this otherwise? Do you know how many times I've sat up all night worrying about whether I tightened a bolt enough or made sure a fuel pipe was properly secured, while my bloody Lancaster was three hundred miles away, twenty thousand feet above Germany? And sure enough the Lanc comes back, and all that worry was for nothing. Or it doesn't, but either way, what can I do about it? Not waste my time worrying over something I can't control. Worry achieves nothing, Arthur, except make a bloke want to walk into a propellor and turn himself into mincemeat.'

'Suppose so. But-'

'But nothing, alright. Now, you feeling better?'

'I feel a bit stupid, to tell you the truth.'

'That's alright. Better stupid than dead, eh?'

Shag clapped his mate around the shoulder and got up. 'Finish your tea, eh? They'll be bringing that Lanc back in a bit and there's bound to be something that'll need fixing.'

Arthur watched Shag head off to the others and light up a fag. He finished the tea and threw the dregs onto the grass and was about to say 'God bless Jimmy' when something made him stop. He smiled, stood up and joined the rest of the crew, scanning the skies for signs of their returning Lanc.

The End of the Tour

Strangely, this time it's different. This time, there's only silence.

When the Lancaster finally settles at its dispersal point, I go through the routine of turning the engines off, as I have done so many times before. One by one the Merlins stutter to a stop, and the sudden silence is overwhelming. This is strange, because there was a time when after an op, the roar of the engines would be replaced by a loud ringing in my ears. This was something the MO diagnosed as Tinnitus, an incurable condition caused, he said, by the constant noise of the engines, but tonight it has gone, and everything seems quiet. But this is the last op of the tour, and things seem different this time.

Once I'm sure that the shutdown procedure is complete, I allow myself a little smile, relieved that I'll never have to perform it again. I pull off my flying helmet and sit back in my seat, allowing my stiff, aching body to relax for the first time in nearly seven hours. As the Skipper I'm always the last to leave my aircraft, and as usual tonight I sit in the cockpit for a minute or so, gathering my thoughts, grateful to be on *terra firma* once again. This time however, with *Stage Door Johnny* completing her tour of thirty ops, the return feels somehow anticlimactic, definitely not the momentous event I'd expected. Eyes closed, I allow sounds to creep into my brain: a few muttered words, the familiar end of shift conversation as the crew unclip their harnesses and pack up, and the clump and scrape of heavy flying boots as they scramble over the main spar towards the tail of the aircraft. There's even a short burst of laughter, a release of pent-up tension and anxiety, and relief that they'll never have to go through this again.

More sounds are filtering in now: the steady tick, ticking of the engines as they cool down, and from outside the aircraft I can hear the voices of the ground crew, calling to each other as they wander around the Lanc, flashing dimmed torches over the flying surfaces, looking for evidence of damage to the wings and fuselage. One of them whistles in amazement at the size of a jagged hole torn in the wing, and another swears, noting its proximity to the fuel tank. As I listen to these strangely comforting sounds, I also become aware of a stillness, now that the constant vibration, which has been shaking every fibre of my body all the way to Germany and back, has ended.

At last I unclip my straps and pull myself up, noticing for the first time the unmistakable coppery smell of blood, which always manages to cut through the all-pervading bomber aromas of oil, gasoline and cordite. Vague memories of an incident flash through my brain: shouted warnings over the intercom of 'Night fighter! Corkscrew left, Skipper!', the sudden stomach-churning sensation as the Lancaster plunged hundreds of feet in a desperate attempt to lose its pursuer, and bright colourful explosions in the cockpit, bizarrely reminiscent of fireworks on bonfire night, before everything was calm again.

I was lucky, I suppose.

I stand at the top of the short exit ladder, breathing in the gloriously fresh smells of an airfield in the early hours of a summer night. I haven't travelled much in my twenty-two years (apart from all these trips to Germany and back) but I'm sure there's nothing like it anywhere else on earth; that unique combination of grass, aviation fuel and, coming from a farm just over the perimeter, the faint whiff of manure. Home, I suppose, and something I will never forget. In the moonlight I can clearly make out the shapes of the other Lancs spread out around the airfield, and looking down I see my crew gathered together, their parachutes slung carelessly on the ground, stretching tired limbs and lighting up welcome fags.

Jumping down off the steps I feel the reassuring firmness of the ground beneath my feet. I have a little ritual which I perform at the end of every op; crouching down I kiss the concrete hardstanding, and say a silent prayer of thanks. The lads all think this very strange, and rather discomforting that their pilot should be so grateful for a safe return, and they usually have a laugh when they see me do this, but not this time. This time it's different. They're huddled together, clouds of cigarette smoke swirling around their inclined heads, talking, I suppose, about the night's operation.

Finally, they turn in my direction, and I follow their gaze, seeing a couple of erks emerge from the Lanc's rear door and pass something heavy in a tarpaulin out to some waiting stretcher bearers. The object is awkward to handle, and they take extreme care not to knock it against anything on the way down. Someone in the crew utters a low curse, and they watch in silence as it is carried away from the bomber towards the waiting blood wagon.

We weren't all so lucky, then?

'We arrived at the target seven minutes late…'

Debriefing. Exhausted crews gathered in a hut, sitting around a table drinking mugs of cocoa and smoking cigarettes, answering the intelligence officer's questions about the raid. He wants to know details of the outward flight, target and return.

'Unexpected headwind-'

'Yes, the other crews have mentioned that.'

'-and dropped all our bombs on the aiming point.'

'You could have flown lower to avoid the headwind…'

'And draw the flak? No thanks.'

'Are you sure you were on the aiming point?'

'Bang on the green flares…'

'Good. Did you get pictures?'

'I saw the photoflash go off then we were out of there. The Skipper didn't hang around - it was pretty hairy, I can tell you.'

'Flak was heavier than we expected on the way in,' I say, filling an awkward pause.

'What about our losses?' The intelligence officer cuts

across me, ignoring my contribution, which I assume he takes as an implicit criticism. 'Anyone see anything?'

The crew reach back into their tired, aching brains as the IO's pen hovers expectantly over the notepad. He can get tetchy if they don't remember all the details of the operation.

'I saw a Lanc go down over the target,' says Les Grayson, our bomb aimer. 'No idea who. Searchlights coned him, didn't stand a chance.'

'Night fighter?'

'Flak, I think.'

'Any 'chutes?'

A shake of the head, and the intelligence officer makes a note. Death and destruction, fear and pain are all described with a neutral, matter-of-factness that says these lads have done this many times before and just want to get into bed now, desperate to let sleep do its magic and wipe away the memory of the night's work.

'The night fighters caught us on the way back.'

'Was that when..?'

'Yes,' pipes up Henry Cole, flight engineer, from Trinidad. 'Somewhere over Holland.'

'West of Eindhoven,' Phil the navigator chimes in.

'Can you be any more precise?'

'No. Sorry. I had other things on my mind...'

The intelligence officer sighs, barely masking his irritation at this blatant unprofessionalism.

'There were two of the bastards. I saw the first, told the Skipper to corkscrew. It was the second one that caught us.' Jimmy Auld, our rear gunner from a village in Perthshire, sprawls in his chair as he recalls the moment he caught a glimpse of the Me 110 night fighter trailing *Stage Door Johnny*.

'How do you know it was a *second* 110? It could have been a single Jerry following you down.'

The rear gunner stares at the intelligence officer. 'Well, I didn't stop to ask the pilots' names and addresses.' No-one laughs. 'The first was a 110. The second an 88.'

'Are you sure?'

105

'It's my job to be sure. Does it matter?'

'It could do. If crews know to expect that night fighters are operating in pairs.'

'Makes no odds to me anyhow,' says Jimmy, leaning his chair back on two legs. 'Next week I'll be putting sprogs through their paces in OTU.'

'Of course, I'd forgotten you all complete your thirty ops tonight. I expect you'll be celebrating in the mess?'

'Well, under the circumstances...'

'Oh yes...'

There's another awkward pause. I'm expecting the lads to be more... well, *happy*, it being the end of their tour, but if anything they seem to be depressed. Like me, I suppose they're feeling a sort of anticlimax. Maybe it's the sense that something special has come to an end. We have been through some unforgettable experiences, learned to trust and depend on one another for our lives, and we have been lucky enough to all survive whatever Jerry has thrown at us. Until tonight, that is; I remember the bloody tarpaulin being carried out of *Stage Door Johnny*, and the dead weight it contained. That is what is on the lads' minds. We have become something of a family over the last six months, after all, flying all these ops together. We'll miss each other now it's all over.

The intelligence officer looks around, sensing that he's pushing his luck with this crew's patience. 'Anything else? Well, goodnight chaps. Oh, and congratulations on completing your tour.'

Chair legs scrape. The crew rise as one and trudge wearily towards the door; all except me, that is. 'I'll catch you up, lads,' I say, but no-one replies; understandably, they can't get out of the room fast enough.

I want to have a private word with the intelligence officer. He's finishing off his notes, still deliberately ignoring my presence. There's the difference of rank between us, I accept; he's an officer and I am only a mere sergeant, but that shouldn't excuse his apparent rudeness. The lads and I have been through thirty of his grillings, sitting exhausted, nerves frayed, after some terrifying ops from which we were sure we would never return; thirty times we have put up with his pedantic schoolmasterly manner when all we wanted to do was sink in a hot bath and restore some feeling to our frozen, aching limbs, or drink ourselves senseless in the mess. Night after night he has asked the same old questions about windspeeds and direction, flying altitude, fuel consumption, enemy defences, bombing patterns, and night after night we have had to put up with his incivility and do our best to answer them.

Until now. The end of the tour.

Now it is my turn to ask him a few questions of my own. I want to know why he never asked us about how it actually felt to be on the end of a flak barrage, seeing those deadly streams of tracer arcing in our direction, seeking out our soft flesh? Perhaps he would be interested to hear about the cold fear you experience when you know there's a night fighter on your tail, deliberately stalking you before choosing the right moment to go in for the kill. And might he not have a question about what we were thinking as we looked down in horror at the dreadful, hellish fires that our bombs were stoking?

I ask him these questions, and many more, quietly, and without anger, and watch for any response on his part, any sign that this stuffed uniform might contain anything resembling a human being. But there is none. Still he ignores me, despite the fact that I am sitting only a few feet away from him. Is this too much for him to deal with? Perhaps he is embarrassed by my expression of feeling, or maybe he's just offended by my impertinence. I can understand that I suppose, but the least he could do is put down his blasted pen and do me the courtesy of listening to what I have to say. So you can imagine my confusion when he finally gets up, and without a word, walks to the door and turns off the lights before leaving the room.

The bastard.

Anyone would think I wasn't even there.

Walking up the corridor to the mess I can hear that the party is in full swing; a crowd of male and female voices shouting to make themselves heard, and someone on the piano thumping out a song, the old Joanna sounding as out of tune as ever. That they are celebrating should come as no surprise, knowing the lads have completed their tour, but given their sombre mood in the debrief I didn't expect them to be partying quite so hard. But one thing we have learned over the tour is to live in the moment; when you have no real control over events, things happen, friends come and go, and you quickly learn to appreciate what you do have, which comes down to one thing – *you are alive*.

Entering, I look around and can't help smiling at the sheer life and energy on display – any thoughts about what happened on the raid are well and truly put to one side as the crews from A and B Flights, joined by a fair sprinkling of WAAFs, admin officers and brass, are letting their hair down, all in the name of celebrating the crew of *Stage Door Johnny's* completed tour.

I remember that I have prepared a few words for this moment – nothing special or too long, the lads would rag me rotten if I dared – but I felt it was important to mark the occasion if we actually made it, and had made a few notes after writing my usual last letters home. Thinking there's no time like the present, I thread my way between the revellers towards the bar, from where I intend to make my little speech. There I wait for a lull in proceedings, and eventually the piano comes to the end of a song; I wait a moment for the applause to die down before calling for attention, as I have a few words to say: 'Okay chaps, bit of quiet please...'

Unsurprisingly, everyone carries on talking, so I raise my voice. 'I say, lads, pipe down while I say a few words...'

But the WAAF sitting at the piano starts banging out another tune, and the party continues. I confess to feeling rather embarrassed, as this is the second time tonight I've been cut dead. It is only as I glance down, to look at the notes I'd written, that I notice I am still wearing my flying kit:

sheepskin lined jacket, and boots. I was obviously so upset by the intelligence officer's earlier behaviour that I must have forgotten to change and freshen up. No wonder everyone here is ignoring me, when they have made such an effort to look smart, on tonight of all nights. I curse myself for my stupidity and selfishness, and then realise that this is only the half of it: the folded-up piece of paper containing my notes is stuck fast by what appears to be dried blood, and there are splashes of blood on my flying kit, and on my hands.

Fragmentary images flash in my brain as I try to work out how the blood got all over me; the memory is dark and confused but I know it must have had something to do with those damned night fighters. But that's no excuse – how could I be so insensitive as to turn up at the party like Banquo's ghost, on the lads' big night? Embarrassed beyond belief, without hanging around to apologise or make my excuses, I push through the happy, red-faced crowd, desperate to get outside.

The cold air hits me as I stagger out from the mess, and I stand there, taking deep breaths, trying to get rid of this overwhelming feeling of sickness and confusion. What is happening to me? Have I finally lost it? They say that some chaps manage to keep it together night after night only to finally lose their nerve right at the very end. Strange, that the mind should work that way. But is that what is happening to me? This certainly isn't how I saw the end of the tour working out.

Perhaps it's for the best that the lads and I go our separate ways now; after all it was the war that brought us together as a crew, and the war that has inevitably split us up again. We will each go off and do our own things, some transferring to instructor duties, or desk jobs; some, God knows why, may even choose to volunteer for another tour.

I don't know what I will do now I don't have to fly; in the short term there is Ruth of course, and as soon as I have tied up the loose ends with the squadron I'll be on the train down to London to see her. For weeks now I have fought off the gnawing fear that I wouldn't make it to the end of my tour by focusing on being with Ruth again. I imagined having breakfast in our little flat, wandering through Soho before she heads off to appear in her show, and hanging around the stage door to take her to a club afterwards, all the things we did when we first met. I became such a regular at the theatre that the other dancers soon called me Ruth's 'Stage Door Johnny', and the name stuck; and it was how R for Roger got her nickname – the lads used to wind me up about going out with an actress, and one of the ground crew painted a garish fantasy of Ruth on the Lanc's nose. It was embarrassing in one way, but in another it gave me quite a boost, and it seemed to bring us luck because *Stage Door Johnny* quickly earned a reputation for having a good solid crew, returning relatively unscathed from ops when others either came back in a very sorry state or not at all. One night, walking along the Embankment to the flat I asked Ruth to marry me, and without hesitation she said 'Yes'. We were married at a pretty church near the station; a small affair, with the crew forming an honour guard of umbrellas as we ran through the pouring rain to the waiting taxi, but after an all-too brief honeymoon in Torquay we immediately fell back into our former, separate lives; Ruth performing in her shows and I appearing nightly over Germany, both of us in the spotlight, so to speak; although I was desperate to stay out of the searching beam.

Truth be told, things have been a bit strained between me and Ruth recently; it's difficult to put a finger on exactly why, but we both know it's there. It was simply wonderful when we first met; we were both on cloud nine, I so pleased to have a glamorous actress on my arm and Ruth proud, I think, to flaunt her brave bomber pilot around town. But with us both being so busy and spending such long periods apart the inevitable strains developed. Ruth, despite her natural optimism and lust for life couldn't help worrying that each time we said goodbye might be our last, which is a terrible weight to put on any marriage. And I succumbed to a kind of jealousy, as each time I remembered first seeing her up there on the stage I couldn't help imagining that any number of men like me must be falling in love with her now. If I'm honest though, there is more to it than that.

I am not the same man I was when I first admired Ruth from the stalls of the Wyndham's Theatre. Thirty exhausting, terrifying, nerve-shedding flights over Germany – not to mention the numerous ops that were scrubbed at the last minute or aborted before we reached the target and therefore not included on the tour - have changed me. The brave, carefree young man of half a year ago has been replaced by a paler version of himself – one less apt to laugh at other's jokes, less comfortable in his own skin, finding it hard to be happy with nothing to do. The strain of losing friends and familiar faces, of never knowing whether each night will be my last, of tensing every nerve and muscle as I see yet another stream of tracer shells snaking up towards me – these things have made me old before my time, and I fear that Ruth won't want to spend the rest of her life with this shadow of a former man. In my darker moments I have even imagined my own death, and seen Ruth's relief that she will be spared that cruel sentence.

But perhaps I am worrying too much, or have been. The tour is over now, things are different for both of us, and everything will work out in the way the fates have decided. It is all too much for my tired, confused brain to deal with now, and when I get back to my billet I fall on my bed, exhausted, and immediately fall into a deep sleep.

Am I dreaming?

I tell myself I must be, because even though it feels so real, I am in the bedroom in our Wandsworth flat, standing over the bed, looking down at Ruth, sleeping. Despite the fact that I am still in full flying kit, I carefully lift back the covers and climb into bed beside her, and put my arms around her body, gently pushing my face into the folds of her chestnut hair, smelling her once again. Something tells me this is the last time I will be with her, and I try desperately not to wake her, wanting to make this moment last forever.

I am safe. I am home.

I whisper gently to Ruth that I am sorry I've been in my own world lately, so distant from her, but that everything is okay now, and she needn't worry any more. I tell her I shouldn't have asked her to marry me when I did – it was selfish, when I knew what I was going to be letting her in for. 'No kind of a life, being married to a bomber pilot,' that's what the boys said, and they were right. It would have been better to wait until I'd completed my tour, then we could have faced a future together with some certainty, but I was afraid. You were so lovely, Ruth, so gentle, warm and reassuring, and I was a frightened kid. I needed someone to tell me it would be alright, that I could go up there and do it all again the next night, and the next; and I did, trying not to think of you all alone, worrying about me, wondering if I would ever come home again.

But it's all over now. I've completed my tour, and we can start again, can't we?

The sudden bright light blinds me. I hold my hand over my eyes, blinking in the harsh glare from the bare electric bulb, and sit up, confused. 'Who turned the bloody light on?' I say, 'Can't you see I'm trying to sleep?'

I can make out someone standing in the doorway of my billet, scanning the room as if looking for something. My confused brain tries to work out what is happening; at first, I assume it must be one of the crew, returned from the party, but as my vision clears I see that this man is an officer, and as we are all NCOs it can't be that. I recognise the man's face; he's the station adjutant, one of those elderly types dragged out of retirement for the war. I've barely spoken a word to him before tonight, only having seen him at briefings and on parade, but what the hell is he doing in my room in the middle of the night? Maybe, my confused brain suggests, he has woken me in the mistaken belief that I'm on ops tonight, and have a day of briefings and flight tests ahead of me. I'm about to put him right when I see him head over to the chest of drawers and start going through my things.

'Wait a minute, sir, what's going on?'

The intruder ignores me, concentrating on separating my belongings out; some things - personal items - he places in a cardboard box and everything else he drops onto the floor. This is too much, so I get up from my bed and approach him, telling him that I was on ops last night and am dog-tired and if only he would tell me what was happening...

But the man carries on with his work, sifting through a pile of letters and postcards from Ruth, and examining the letters I wrote to her and my parents before take-off yesterday. These are tossed carelessly into the cardboard box, along with a photograph of Ruth, my travel alarm and the watch I got on my 21st birthday. The man is methodical, impersonal, unembarrassed about being caught in this blatant act of burglary, and determined to ignore me.

The door opens and another man walks in – an NCO this time, who I've never seen before – and at a nod from the adjutant this man pulls the sheets and blanket off my bed, throwing them into a pile on the floor.

'Not right, is it, sir?' says the NCO.

'What isn't?' says the other.

'Well, I mean, to end your tour like this.'

'Damned bad luck, I agree.'

'I always pity the girl back home.'

'Oh, she's a pretty thing,' says the Adjutant, repressing a cough. 'I daresay she'll soon find someone else.'

Find someone else? No, you don't understand, I say, I know that things have been difficult between Ruth and me but now I've completed my tour I can spend more time with her, we can sort through the difficulties, maybe even think about kids. Anyway, why on earth would Ruth need to find someone else, unless..?

'Right, bag that lot, will you?' says the adjutant. 'I've got a couple of letters to write before breakfast. If it's a nice day I want to get some time in on the garden.'

'Unless..? They can't mean... Surely not...'

The NCO gathers the clothing up and the adjutant moves towards the door, carrying the cardboard box, which suddenly, and inexplicably, flies out of his hands, spreading the contents – the letters, photographs and other mementoes of the dead pilot's life – across the floor. Afterwards, both men would confess to friends that as the box flew out of the adjutant's hands they could have sworn they heard something like a man's voice, shouting No! but as there is no-one else in the room neither man wishes to appear spooked, and so nothing is said. The NCO, his face distinctly paler than before, quickly finishes gathering up the dead pilot's clothing and bedding, and leaves; the adjutant replaces the contents of the box, holding it firmly under his arm, and takes a last look around the empty room.

The light is turned off and the door is closed.

The end of the tour.

L for Lanc

It's a beautiful sunny afternoon in late May, and I'm sitting alone in the churchyard, waiting for her to arrive.

High up in the tower of St Mary Magdalene, bells chime the half hour and I look at my watch, a little anxious. It's 3.30, and she's not here yet. I take a deep breath and check my watch again. Don't worry, you haven't missed her. Too early yet. 3.35 was the arrangement. She'll be on time, she always is.

Knowing I've got a few minutes, I look around and contemplate the scene laid out before me: a large tree-filled public garden, formerly the church graveyard, surrounded by the familiar low, red-brick buildings that characterise the Georgian centre of Newark. I say former graveyard, as some years ago it was cleared of the old grey-slate headstones which marked the resting place of dead men, women and children for hundreds of years. Sad to think that their one opportunity to say, 'I lived here, and my time on earth will not go unmarked,' has now gone; their precious, fragile immortality erased on the nod of some mundane parish works committee. I find myself wondering what the ghosts of these folk might have thought as they felt the ground of their once-peaceful resting places shake and tremble to the sudden violence of the mechanical diggers; how did they feel when they heard the council workmen, laughing and joking as they pulled up the magnificent and beautifully carved headstones, before re-laying them nearby to provide cheap, functional groundcover around the church? And I wonder if their bodies remain mingled with the soil beneath my feet, or if they were respectfully disinterred and buried elsewhere, and whether anyone will ever know, or care.

I realise I'm thinking about death again, and the nagging fear that all my years on this earth won't amount to much more than a hill of beans in the scheme of things sends a slight chill through my body. Who will remember me? What was it all for? And was it worth it? I take a deep breath, trying to clear my mind of these and other hopeless and circular thoughts, and put a smile on my face as I look around at the churchyard.

I can't deny that it's a pleasant place; very green, with massive yew, oak and horse chestnut trees providing a dappled shade for the squirrels that chase each other between the low privet hedges. Birdsong fills the air – blackbirds mostly, and the cheerful, flinty chirp of house sparrows. There are couples walking through the gardens, while others sit, like me, on benches, enjoying the welcome sun as they chat. Not far off, a couple of teenage girls sit cross-legged together, sharing secrets, and a young mother keeps an eye on her toddler, as he discovers the joys of grass and sunshine, with legs that seem to run all by themselves. It's been a long winter, cold and miserable, and the warm sun is an unexpected bonus today. A sign that things are changing.

But where is she?

The faint sound of an aircraft engine breaks through the voices and the birdsong. I scan the sky, peering through the tracery of leaves, tilting my good ear in the direction of the drone, and sure enough, a few seconds later a small white aeroplane moves slowly across the cloudless blue sky.

I look at my watch again. 3.36. She is late now. She must have encountered an unexpected delay. Maybe she's been held up at a previous engagement, hanging around a little longer than planned, giving her admirers an extra free look before heading my way.

I see a figure emerge from behind the ivy-covered wall and past the leant-up slate headstones, into the churchyard. It's an old man, older than me at any rate, and my eye was caught by the distinctive blue workman's overalls he's wearing. As he ambles towards me, I imagine he's probably a mechanic, or an engineer, some sort of artist maybe – he'll be doing a hands-on job at any rate. He's coming from the direction of a small workshop I noticed recently, which has a little plaque fitted above the door informing visitors about the hole, high up in St Mary's spire, which was supposedly left by a cannon ball, fired by the Parliamentarian forces from Beacon Hill during the Civil War. They weren't aiming at the church, presumably, but if they were it surely ranks as one of the earliest and best examples of precision bombing. My guess is that they were aiming at the Governor's House on the other side of the market square, or, like the Russian forces currently besieging towns in Ukraine, it was all just part of an attempt to terrorise the local population. Anyway, perhaps this old guy in the blue overalls has come from the workshop and knows more about the story. But before I can pursue that thought, suddenly my heart leaps and all my senses are alert as a familiar sound slowly grows and fills the sky.

Merlins! There's no mistaking that low, full-throated roar. Nothing like it exists in the skies today. I look around, shielding my eyes from the bright sun, straining to spot where she is, but I can't see her. I almost expect the birds in the trees to suddenly stop and listen, and all the people to look up, this is such a rare and important moment, but they carry on, oblivious. I'm the only one who seems to know or care about what is happening.

The roar is building, but I still can't see her. I don't want to stand, thinking that I'll appear ridiculous, like an excited little boy, but that's exactly how I feel now. The man in the blue overalls is only a few yards away from me. He lifts his head and nods me a brief alright, but I'm so busy scanning the skies that I don't respond. And then just behind him, I see her.

The Lancaster.

Her unmistakable silhouette hangs low over the rooftops as she comes out of a gentle banking turn, perhaps half a mile away, hanging masterfully in the air like some enormous black Pterodactyl. I can't tell whether she's heading towards me or flying in the opposite direction. I'm holding my breath and feeling that same excited boyhood thrill I get every time I see a warbird, a Hurricane or Spitfire, but which is

117

doubled, no quadrupled, when I see the Lancaster.

'There's the Lanc,' I blurt involuntarily, and the man in the overalls stops and turns to look. I could have been pointing out someone famous. 'Just over the roofline, there.' I point, and with his hand shielding his eyes he eventually sees her.

'Ah, yes...'

We both watch in silence, united in a kind of communion for a few moments, no more than ten seconds really, before the Lancaster disappears from view, followed a few seconds later by the sound of her Merlins. It's suddenly quiet again, and as if the Lanc had never really been there at all, but a mere ghost.

'She were supposed to be here at 3.35,' he says. Like me, he must have read in the *Advertiser* that the Battle of Britain Memorial Flight's Lancaster was due to fly over the County Showground this afternoon. Today is the first County Show since Lockdown was lifted, and the organisers wanted to mark its return with something special. You don't get much more special than the Lanc. I bet they had a good crowd.

'I thought she might give us a show and fly over the town,' he says, and he smiles, acknowledging our shared admiration of the Lanc, before ambling on towards the market square. I'm pleased to note that he too refers to the Lanc as she.

Maybe she will, I think, and I remain alone on the bench, hopeful that the familiar silhouette will emerge for another flypast. I feel strangely exhilarated, as if I've emerged from some sort of fugue or dream, but looking around I realise that no-one else in the graveyard saw what I saw, heard what I heard, felt what I felt. They carry on with their conversations, their playing, their handholding and secret-sharing, completely oblivious to the brief but significant communion I've just experienced beneath the lovely old spire of St Mary Magdalene.

But she doesn't return. I reason that as she was late, if only by a few minutes, the flight engineer will have calculated her available fuel down to the last minute and won't want to take any chances on her return home to Coningsby. She's old and frail, and the crew can't afford to take too many liberties with her. And I shouldn't be greedy. At least I got a brief glimpse of her again.

And there will be another time, I hope.